Rules to
Die by

Rules to Die by

JANETTE ANDERSON

BearManor Media

2014

Rules to Die by
© 2014 Janette Anderson
Janette Anderson Entertainment
WGA 1699527

For information, address:

BearManor Media
P. O. Box 71426
Albany, GA 31708

bearmanormedia.com

Typesetting and layout by John Teehan

Cover by Lori M.

Published in the USA by BearManor Fiction

ISBN—1-59393-559-5
978-1-59393-559-7

Dedicated to Bob,
with love

Chapter 1

Philip Andrea Vega wasn't aware that half the household had been at his bedside keeping a vigil since the gunshot incident in the cemetery. If it had not been for Alex and Patrick, Philip would be dead from the bullet fired from his own gun. They had tackled him as he pulled the trigger to try to end his own life... not part of the main plan, just Vega's own intention after he buried Emma... or thought he had.

Alex had grabbed the gun, turning it away from Vega's face, sending the bullet into his boss's shoulder. Patrick reached the gravestone right after Alex, leaving the engine running on EV1, Emma's Mercedes, and between them they forced the Don of the powerful Vega family to the ground, blood streaming from the gaping hole the bullet left.

And now he lay there in his luxurious oversized bed, his upper body swathed in bandages where the bullet had pierced through his shoulder, chipping bones on its way and clipping his face as it departed his body. But he had been lucky... he had lived. Not his intention. His intention was to die to join his beloved Emma in the grave that she lay in or the one he thought she did.

Violent dreams and morphine clouded his mind. He fought against the noise of guns, fought hard against the morphine and any other drugs still in his system, while pictures of Emma flashed through his mind. He could see her, touch her, hold her, and make love to her. And he yelled out for her. But she couldn't hear him and he lost her in the immeasurable clouds of despair and pain he was in.

"Any movement today?" asked the older doc, who had been with the Vega family for years. Leaning over Philip, he felt for his pulse. It was steady now, unlike the previous days. The doc took that as a good sign. "His color is improving. Try talking to him, playing him music, anything." He paused, almost frightened to ask. "Did you find her yet?"

Patrick's voice was quiet, scared that his father might hear, yet knowing he couldn't. "No...no sign. He doesn't even know the truth... that's the stupid part. All he could remember before he shot himself was that Emma was gone. He kept repeating that Marc had killed Emma, and he and Mac killed Marc. After that, to him, it was a blur. Something about Emma dying. Marc shot her..." Patrick looked up at the doc from his seat on the bed in the same soiled clothes of yesterday, his eyes moist with tears, tired from days of sitting with his father.

"But it was someone else's gravestone you found him at..." the doc mused, stroking his white whiskers, thinking out loud more than anything.

"Yes, it was...somehow in his mind when they took Emma he thought she was dead. The blow to his head in the room that day, plus the drugs they gave him, made him lose memory of reality." Patrick blinked back tears, and tried to change the subject a little. "He will recover, right?"

"Physically, yes....the wound will heal, except for maybe a small scar on the side of his face."

"And mentally?" Patrick dreaded the reply.

"Depends when he wakes up what the last thing he remembers is. If it's before or at the hotel in Santa Barbara then all will be well... let's hope for the best. Did the 'family' find Marc yet?"

"No...but when we find him, he will die in such a way that he will wish that my father had killed him the day he found out he planned to kidnap Emma!" And in Patrick Vega's eyes there was hate that terrified the old doc, a hate that stemmed from being the son of the father who had so much power and an ongoing lust to kill. And a man right now that was fighting to stay alive.

Chapter 2

Jillie Jennings sat in the small blue rented car waiting for the large iron gates to open. She was nervous and it showed, her hands shaking on the steering wheel. She knew it was crazy to feel like this. Jillie had been a nurse for eight years now… in a hospital that was, not a private nurse in a reputed mob family's home. She peeked into her driving mirror, turning round to get her best side. Slim faced and tanned, she felt a tad more lipstick was appropriate. Fluffing her long brown hair out to make her features more prominent, she thought she looked okay.

"Why the heck am I bothering? The man's unconscious, and he would hardly notice me if he was conscious, not after a wife like his…" The thought stopped her in her tracks and she glanced up as the tall iron gates opened to let her into the sprawling grounds that seemed to spring forth with bodyguards in place of rose bushes.

Cleared there, she drove down the long tarmac drive to the house that the Vega family called home…one that had been handed down from fathers to sons for decades and one that would carry on that way. The house was impressive to say the least. Winter ivy clung to the walls and a giant wooden door was the gateway to heaven or hell: whichever way you looked at it. For some reason, Jillie hadn't expected the mansion to be quite so big, so overwhelming; so much so that she almost turned the car round and drove back the way she came.

"This is silly. You are a big girl… just do it! What's the family going to do? The instructions were clear enough." Jillie was more than nervous, even though she had been well briefed about the situation. She was there to look after Philip Vega until he regained consciousness… or not. How hard could that be? It wasn't until a little bird had told her that he wasn't just in the movie business: that he was involved in another kind of business that wasn't quite on the right side of the law that she became nervous.

And now there was no time to change her mind. The large door opened and a tall, dark-haired man strode out to meet her. Alex, one of Vega's personal bodyguards, had been assigned to greet her and fill her in on the situation in hand; after all, he had been there in the cemetery. He waited till she stopped the car and she climbed out, bringing her bag with her.

Alex towered over Jillie. "Ms. Jennings, my name is Alex." He nodded his head to her and put his hand out to take her overnight-bag that she had retrieved from the front seat of her car.

She figured she would get the rest of her things later, and handed it to him. "Thank you, Alex…" She went to say more but was stopped by the sight of a man that she thought looked the epitome of gangster who went to the back of her car and stood looking at it.

"Keys," was the only word he uttered in a graveled voice and, as she would later find out, this was Rossi, someone you didn't mess around with.

Jillie obediently tossed him the keys and he opened the trunk and pulled out her case, while also checking that's all she had in there. Satisfied, he took the case and walked with giant strides of a tall man back into the house.

"Don't mind Rossi. He is always like that. But as you can see we do have a lot of security here. I will fill you in on the rules over dinner. And now I will show you the part of the house that will concern you the most," and he escorted her through the door and into the seemingly endless halls of the house.

She gazed around her. In all her twenty-seven years on the planet, she had never seen a house like this one. Wealth positively oozed from every crack and crevice from the foundation to the roof, and she wondered what secrets it also housed. She shivered.

"Cold, Ms. Jennings, or may I call you JJ for short?"

"Why not, everyone else does…Is this all one home?" she asked, knowing that was a stupid question.

Alex was almost amused. "You mean does all this belong to Mr. Vega? Yes, it does. The whole family lives here, including Mr. Patrick and the younger Vega children. You will meet them all at dinner. But now I want to show you your room. It is right next to Mr. Vega's. You are on call 24/7 except when one of us is with him. Understood ?"

"Yes, Sir…"

"You don't have to call me *Sir*…only Mr. Vega earned that title," he paused, thinking, "And perhaps now Mr. Patrick." Alex shuddered at the thought. "You have been thoroughly checked out and you are well suited for this job, and your job is to keep Mr. Vega alive… at any cost," and Alex said the last words with far more emphasis than was needed.

By now they had reached the suite of the said Mr. Vega, and Alex turned the handle of the door next to his room.

"This is your room, JJ… mine is the other side of yours, and to the other side of Mr. Vega's is his personal bodyguard who is also on call 24/7. He will introduce himself to you later." He paused and looked at her face. "I am not sure how much you know…Mr. Vega is the well known movie star that every woman loves, but he also a very astute business man… and what goes on in this household, stays in this household…are you very clear on that…"

"Yes, Sir… I mean, yes, Alex. May I see Mr. Vega?" and she took her small bag from him and pushed it just inside the now open door to her large and airy room. She glanced rather quickly inside and did a double take, almost stunned at the incredible size of the room. Exploring it later would be an adventure.

"Of course. You will find your large suitcase near your closet and anything that you need there. If it's not, then let me know. There is a phone by your bed. Dial 3 for my line." Once more he paused. "And now I will show you to Mr. Vega. Please do not be shocked by all the security in the room. It's for all of our protection, but mostly for Mr. Vega," and Alex turned the door handle and led her through the large private lounge towards the inner bedroom. Alex knocked gently on the door and a voice answered.

"Come in, Alex..." Patrick Vega called the bodyguard into the room. He had been sitting talking to his father and had heard the car noises outside his father's window. He stood up, letting his hand release his father's fingers, ones that he rested back on the crisp white sheets, and moved towards the door.

"Ms. Jennings, I presume. I am Patrick Vega and as you can clearly see, that is my father, Philip Vega... and as far as the outside world is concerned... he didn't survive the gunshot..."

JJ put her hand out to shake the out stretched hand in front of her. The handshake was firm and matter of fact, as was the demeanor of man in front of her. He was all business, very attractive to look at with deep brown eyes and jet black hair, but all business none-the-less. And then she looked at the 'dead' man lying in the oversized very-elegant bed, bandages covering his upper body and one down the side of his face... and as she looked at him JJ knew her life had changed forever.

Chapter 3

Vega lay totally unaware JJ was in the room, even unaware that his son and Alex were there. He couldn't feel anything; only pain… the one in his heart. Why wake up? He knew Emma wasn't there. He knew she was gone and Emma was the only thing he wanted in life. Suddenly, there was a smell of perfume. Just a hint, unfamiliar to him… it wasn't Emma's. He couldn't place it but maybe he wasn't so far under as he thought. Perhaps tomorrow he would try to wake up… maybe.

His eyelashes fluttered just momentarily and JJ could not help notice how long and black they were and how ultra masculine this man was. There was a bandage taped across his cheek and his chest was swathed in them, but still one could see his ripped body and the black hair that curled down towards the pit of his stomach. She traced the lines of his body under the sheets, her eyes like magnets drawn to him in a second, while his breathing was steady and his chest rose and fell …and Alex saw the instant fascination.

"JJ is here for as long as it takes for Mr. Vega to recover. Her room is next door and she knows she is on call 24/7." He paused. "Dinner is at seven, Mr. Patrick," Alex stated, setting the example for JJ to follow. "And now, Sir, if you would like, I can show her what she needs to do in here for the boss."

"Fine, that's fine. I should visit with the children before dinner." His mind was elsewhere and it showed. Patrick looked down at himself.

"And maybe take a shower since we now have company." His clothes needed more than just changing. He did, however, notice the way JJ was looking at his father and smiled a tiny smile to himself. It had always been his father that had drawn the women in the Vega household. "Seven, you said? I will be there," and twenty-seven-old year Patrick Vega disappeared from the room closing the door firmly behind him.

Alex waited until Patrick was well out of earshot. "He has a lot on his mind, and you are here to take some of that load from him and all of us. You think you can manage that?"

JJ knew he was watching her reaction. "I think I can handle that very well. As you said I was cleared and checked out before I came here. I just didn't expect... I , er," and she stumbled in her speech.

"Let me finish that for you. You didn't expect Mr. Vega to look like this, right?"

"Right!" She hadn't expected it all right, but not in the way Alex meant it. "Would you mind showing me where everything is kept? And I am assuming that there is a doctor that comes in most days..."

"Every day at eleven..." and Alex escorted her to the table where there were a dozen bandages and anything she might happen to need. "Bathroom is right through that door, and if you need anything else you let me know..." As he finished speaking, the door opened to the bedroom and Mac, the very personal bodyguard, entered.

Mac was stern, not as forthcoming as Alex, and viewed JJ with deep blue eyes that she figured might hold menacing thoughts behind them. She immediately straightened up and waited for an introduction.

"Mac this is JJ. She will be here... for as long as she is needed."

Mac put his hand out to shake her hand and as he did his leather jacket opened slightly and in plain sight, revealing a gun tucked down the front of his jeans. He knew it was there and he didn't try to hide it. He wanted the girl to see it. Alex was the good guy... and Mac wasn't.

"Nice to meet you. You come recommended and you will no doubt earn your pay. I'm sure Alex has shown you where things are. I will stay here till dinner and then join you all then," and they were dismissed by the dominant Mac Hunter, bodyguard deluxe in the Vega household, who escorted them to the door.

JJ and Alex stepped into the hallway.

"Wow…is he always like that?" asked the girl, somewhat frightened by the more than dominant attitude that Mac displayed.

"Yes… he has to be. It's his job… and now, you know where your room is. I will meet you by your door at six-forty-five and escort you to dinner," he paused, "and do not wander around the house on your own. It would not be wise."

And with that JJ was left on her own to wonder just what kind of world she had entered into. She turned the handle into the lavish bedroom, one she could only dream about, and disappeared inside to check it out.

Alex went back into Vega's room. He didn't knock, just slipped quietly in to join Mac.

Mac turned slightly away from the bed and moved towards Alex.

"She settling in okay?" Mac asked, not really looking at Alex.

"I think so. Did you notice the way she was looking at the boss?"

"I did…but then every woman that comes here does that….but, yes, I saw. Maybe keep an eye on that."

Mac proceeded to sit down and look at Vega. Even with bandages and the obvious scar, he was still an extremely handsome man, one whose features and coloring they would need to change when he was awake… if that ever happened.

Mac thought back a week or two. It should have been him that had been knocked out and drugged. Instead it was his boss and he, and Alex, were partly to blame for the situation that was now taking place… and that's why they kept watch 24/7.

When Philip walked back through the hotel bedroom with room service, Marc had been waiting, gun at Emma's head. He had her perched on the side of the lavish Jacuzzi…where she and Philip had just made love. She wore hardly any clothes and Marc slid the.357 down her face. The look of terror in his young pregnant wife's eyes told Philip what he needed to know. They were the last thing he saw as the blow struck him from behind and he fell face down onto the cold hard floor, out to the world. As a needle went into his arm, he couldn't feel it. Cocaine filled his system as Marc laughed and Vinnie didn't even bother to see how much he emptied into Vega. It should have been enough to OD on and Vega would have, had he not been as strong as he was.

Mac and Alex had raced from their room to the aid of their boss almost too late, and found him there on the floor and Emma gone and that's what Philip Vega knew… that Emma was gone.

Chapter 4

Jillie scuffed the carpet just slightly with her high heels. She thought they would be okay for dinner… she hoped, and waited patiently at the door for Alex. Glancing at her watch, she was just a little early, and smoothed her dress, taking any creases from it. Maybe she would peek in Mr. Vega's room and maybe not. She was thinking about her room and how resplendent it was when a voice interrupted her.

"Ready for dinner, JJ?" Alex glanced at her. "Formal is good. I should have told you but you guessed correctly. Nice dress," he commented, really meaning it. "Okay, let's go so you can meet the rest of the family. It's rather a large turnout for dinner."

As they approached the room, JJ could hear the noise of children. Her heart warmed. One day she wanted children. First she had to find a man. There had been plenty but not the right one so far… As she was contemplating this, a small child dressed in a pretty pink dress came bursting through the doorway. The child was gorgeous. Long blonde hair but with darker looks, a cute turned up nose and deep brown eyes that looked up at JJ with expectancy. Then she looked away and disappeared back into the room, apparently not finding whom she wanted to find outside the door.

"That was Philipa, or Pip, as Mr. Vega calls her. She is his youngest child."

"Mr. Patrick's child?" she asked, rather surprised.

"Not Patrick's…Mr. Philip Vega. The boss's youngest for now. He and Emma…" and he stopped dead. Bad move on two counts. Wasn't this girl's business to know and also they hadn't found Emma. "I'll introduce you…" and Alex ushered her through the open door.

The talking promptly stopped and a dozen faces looked up from the over-decorated table, one that was crowned with a chandelier.

JJ stopped dead. No one had prepared her for this. No amount of preparation could have forewarned her of the faces now staring at her. As she looked around the table, Alex introduced her.

"This is Jillie Jennings. We will call her JJ," and Alex took her by the shoulders and propelled her in front of him. "Starting on the left…Rossi, whom you met very briefly today… glue that holds this house together. Next to him is Pauli…someone that will be there whenever you need him."

Pauli nodded his head to her and took a long drag on his smoke. She guessed he was about fifty, maybe more, very attractive and very Italian. Then came Patrick, who seemed more than amused at her lack of confidence. He smiled at her and uttered a greeting while trying to hold on to the little girl who was attempting to climb onto his knee.

Alex continued. "Next are the twins. Orry and Daniel… you'll figure out which one is which. Good boys for the most part," and Alex smiled at them and continued speaking. "Donna is along side them… she, er, is a friend of the Vega family," and Alex skipped on by Donna who was Marc's ex and was obviously very pregnant. "JJ, this is Mac, whom you met earlier. Mac runs the household and everyone in it with an iron fist. His bite is worse than his bark…" and Alex laughed along with the rest of the table.

It took JJ a moment to realize what he had said. She shuddered. He scared her, even with his blonde hair and blue eyes; there was definitely something very menacing about him. He was someone you would not cross…twice. He leaned back in the chair and viewed her almost suspiciously. And they passed on by to the rest of the table. JJ heard their names and took it all in, but her eyes darted between Patrick and Mac. She wasn't quite sure why only that Mac scared her. He was Mr. Vega's right-hand man… an extension of him and perhaps was on to her already. Maybe this wasn't such a good idea being in this household. She smiled politely as the introductions were finished and then let herself be escorted to the seat offered.

Alex pulled the chair out for her and sat down next to her. He could almost feel the tension between her and Mac by the looks the personal guard was giving her. It amused Patrick but also concerned him. Mac was usually right on his takes of people.

Dinner was polite. Lasted an hour, much wine flowed and JJ made sure she drank nothing but water. As usual, the meal was Italian, a kind of spicy food that she loved. Soon it would be time to start work. She watched the little girl blow kisses goodnight to her brothers and then the two younger boys disappeared. Alex had started her on the nightshift feeling it would be the easiest for her.

"Ok, JJ. Let's go. Time to work... Mac?" It was a question, like 'are you coming with us,' but with one word.

And Mac rose from his chair. "Patrick," and Mac tipped his head just slightly and left the room with Alex and JJ. He never said another word; just led the way to Vega's room. Mac had the feeling that he and Mr. Vega had seen this woman somewhere before. But only his boss could verify this.

After quickly changing her clothes, she was ushered into the room, and once again viewed her patient. This was to be her world for as long as it took. Changing his bandages when the doctor didn't, making sure the I.V's were doing their job, and checking on Philip Vega to make sure that he was comfortable and also to make sure that Don Andrea did not wake up sooner than some folks wanted him to. A sleeping Don or even a dead one would benefit a lot of people right now... and that was her job to keep it like that.

Chapter 5

"**L**eave a guard in that room at all times, Alex… there is something about JJ that does not ring true. I've seen her before. Can't put my finger on it…the boss was there but he can't help us at present. I sure wish he would wake up, even show signs that he wants to. I thought that a woman being around might help that process…" Mac's voice tailed off. Loyal to the bitter end… and a man who would give his life for Philip Vega.

"I saw the way you were watching her. No idea where you have seen her before? Maybe one of his past dalliances?" Alex stopped mainly because of the stare that Mac was giving him. "I meant before Emma came along…"

"I know what you meant…maybe, but somehow I don't think it's even that, even though it was hard to keep track of them all… And Emma, we have to find her before he comes back to reality, or both you and I will be out of a job…plenty of men want to work for the Vega family…always have and always will…I'll check back in the room before I turn in. Tomorrow Patrick wants to hold a meeting… with all of us. Noon," and with that Mac turned on his heel and left Alex standing there thinking there might be some things that Mac never told him.

Mac slept badly that night. Once or twice he almost had JJ in the dream and then the thoughts were gone. He woke in a sweat, pulled a T-shirt over his head and went in running pants to Vega's door. He stopped before turning the handle of his boss's room. He was being paranoid… wasn't he? She wouldn't be here if she wasn't for real. And

Patrick would have known her. He had met most of his father's *friends*. What if she was one of Marc's friends…couldn't be? Now he *was* being paranoid and he returned to his room and lay there watching the ceiling fan spun round and round until he drifted back to sleep.

Noon seemed to come fast. Breakfast was a hurried affair. Children sent with armed guards to school and the library seemed to be abuzz with the Italian clan. JJ had been relieved and was now in her room asleep, and a guard was posted outside it making sure she stayed there.

Patrick took his father's chair, reluctantly, but he took it. It was way too big for him… and he knew it. To his right sat Mac and the other side was Rossi. They cut an imposing picture all dressed in black as they sat in leather chairs.

"I have called this meeting today to see what else we can do to find Emma. It has been almost a week now, a week too long and there is no sign of her, no ransom note or any sign of my brother…" Patrick hesitated. Marc was not his brother in any way, shape, or form. He was supposedly his cousin. No… he wasn't even that. No one seemed to know who Marc's father was…least of all Marc, and that was the problem. One thing was clear. The night in the Biltmore, when he and Vinnie filled his father with drugs, Marc took Emma away to make her his own… and Patrick had no doubt he had done that by now one way or another!

He continued. "If the Don wakes and Emma is not found, heads will roll… you all know that, including mine. What we know is that Marc and Vinnie took her. For Vinnie it was payback time for my father killing his brother. For Marc…" and Patrick stopped. He, also, had never stopped loving his father's wife and for him this was hard.

Mac saw it and stepped in. To him, Emma was like his kid sister. But he knew how much Patrick loved his father's wife… and how he also would give his life for Emma and especially for his father.

"If the Don was awake he would have every man looking for her. He knows Marc better than we do. So we have to play by different rules than he would. Mr. Vega can contact people we cannot. But what we can do is send people to Florida and Vegas. Vinnie Carbina was seen yesterday in Vegas surrounded as you might imagine by a host of guards. Vinnie is not a rich young man; therefore, someone is bankrolling him and Marc. I think that all Marc saw was a chance to get Emma and get rid of the boss. Of course we know he failed to do that, but the outside world … they are not so sure if Don Andrea is alive or dead. And that's how it must stay."

There were rumblings round the table as the older men agreed and the younger ones wanted blood.

"And what if we don't find her, Mac? What if Marc is with another Don? Only the boss can confront them…and right now he can't help, and if he does confront them then they know he is not dead," stated Pauli.

"Rock and a hard place. Unless…" and Mac looked at Patrick. "If your father was dead… you would be the next Don…and we could back you. You would have the right to ask," Mac said quite calmly.

"I can't do that…I can't take my father's place just like that…" Patrick was shocked that Mac would even suggest it.

"But it would imply you have taken over and that your father is deceased," added Pauli.

"Forget it! You're insane!" Patrick yelled at Mac.

"You want to find Emma, don't you?" said Mac in a louder voice. "*You* more than anyone," was said with a little too much emphasis.

"You know I do," and Patrick knew the secret was out. "Send soldiers tomorrow. Give him another couple of days before we try anything like you suggest. Then I might agree…" and Patrick turned away and left the room, returning to his father's room.

Pauli stood up and moved his chair back. "It might work. Better if it was Don Andrea though. Not so sure Patrick is ready for that…"

"Neither am I, Pauli… neither am I. Let's hope that the boss wakes. Doc doesn't know why he is still like he is. End of the week, I think we should try something. I have an idea. Yesterday when the nurse was in there, his eyelids fluttered just slightly like he sensed there was a female in the room. If we let her stay in the room with him on her own, except for the guard. Let her talk to him. Wear Emma's perfume…"

"Patrick's right. You are insane!" Alex wasn't so quiet.

"Or Donna…" Rossi said in a low tone.

"What?! Donna?" Mac was astounded.

"They had a brief encounter years ago. You remember. One Christmas when they were both drunk." Rossi had been there that year, but the comment was a little sarcastic.

"It was an accident…" Mac added.

"Yeah, I know it was. And it's just as crazy as your idea! But at least we know Donna likes him and is not going to hurt him." Rossi took a long puff on his cigarette and stared at Mac.

"Good point. JJ likes him, too. But not sure we can trust her. I think she might be a plant. I assume her cell was taken from her?" asked Mac.

Rossi nodded yes. "Any communication is disabled. She can't contact anyone till she leaves here."

"Then we will give her a few days here; let her try this idea out. But she doesn't leave this house. Period!" And Mac, too, left the room. Meeting was ended, and JJ's future now hung in the balance.

Chapter 6

Patrick watched his father through the afternoons. He could never step into his shoes and now he knew it… and it scared him. Maybe Mac's idea wasn't so crazy. He certainly couldn't wake him up. Maybe a woman could…

The days of the week slipped by and JJ felt she was in control. Everything was going to plan. She felt secure with Mac now and certainly with Vega.

The end of the week came around and Patrick sat there propped in the chair only half-awake his mind wandering.

The door opened behind him and JJ came through the doorway. She looked a little shocked that Patrick was sitting there this late in the afternoon.

"Come in, JJ. I was just about to leave. I am sure my father prefers female company to mine any day. Here, take my seat," and Patrick got up and let JJ sit where he had been. Then he braved it. "Touch his hand. I think it's much warmer than yesterday. His whole body is up a notch. See what you think," and he watched her hesitate. Maybe they were all wrong. Or maybe because he himself was standing there was putting her off.

"You are right, Sir…" and she slid her hand along Vega's arm, her fingers feeling his flesh as they went. There was definite warmth, meaning that his body was responding to touch. "Maybe a little too warm. Perhaps he needs another shot of morphine…"

"No, I think we should lay off that. See how he does without it for a day. Doc said to try…" Doc had said no such thing. This was Patrick's idea. And the theory was about to be put to the test. Nurse JJ was a little too free with the drugs.

"As you say. I'll stay here and watch out for him," and she made herself comfortable in the bedside chair.

"I'll see you tomorrow, JJ… we have business away from the house tonight. Anything you need, Alex will help you out," 'and keep and eye on you,' thought Patrick.

When Patrick had left the room, JJ leaned closer. "Damn!" Now she couldn't keep him under. If she couldn't do that then she had to distract him. Shouldn't be too hard with a man like Vega. She watched his chest rise and fall, and his breathing became better by the minute, and he seemed to be settling into a more peaceful sleep. Nothing she could do now except watch her charge and change the bandages for him. She looked round the bedroom. There was more than a hint of a female there. It was full of Emma. JJ rose from her chair and moved to the dresser. Perfumes, makeup and jewelry graced the vanity units. All things she could never afford. Without even thinking JJ sprayed some of the most expensive perfume onto her wrists. It wafted in the air and she tried to fan it away with her hands. Not a smart move. There was a noise outside the door and JJ returned to her seat. She looked down at Philip lying there and for a second his eyelashes flickered and opened just for a second.

JJ almost jumped out of the chair.

Philip tried to focus. It was difficult. A blur. He could smell Emma. But he couldn't see her. He had felt a touch on his arm. But it wasn't her. And then he blinked…hard. He could see someone there in his room and he could feel pain in his side. Searing pain and he wondered just what kind of hell he was in.

"Emma…" Vega whispered. "Is that you?" and still he tried to focus.

It was then that Alex came into the room and with him he brought Donna. He had come to try out what Mac had suggested. Both he and Donna rushed to the bedside.

"What happened? Is he awake…?" Alex looked at his boss.

"He is murmuring his wife's name." JJ was nervous. This was not what she was supposed to do. She was there to make sure he didn't wake. All she had done was used the perfume…

Alex could smell it. He'd know that scent anywhere. "How did you know to do that?" The plan wasn't in action yet.

"I'm sorry. It was an accident..." and JJ was scared. She may not have had a cell phone to let anyone know he was awake... but know they would and now she knew that she had to get out of there. A few days on the job and she had failed...miserably. Or she could come clean and tell them why she was really there.

Philip spoke again and this time he raised his hand and grabbed the arm he thought was Emma. He couldn't see her properly and as he touched her arm Philip knew it wasn't his wife. He immediately let go.

Alex stepped in. "Boss... it's me Alex. Can you hear me?" He leaned down to him.

"Yeah. I hear you. You are kind of blurred." Philip turned his head just slightly and there was pain. "God damn that hurt! What is happening here and where is Emma? I smelled her perfume... Emma," he called out, not knowing where to look.

"She's not here, boss." Alex turned to Donna. "Go get Mac, NOW... and see if Patrick is still here..."

Donna nodded and fled from the room to find them.

"Boss...lie still. You have I.V's in you. Please lie still," and Alex put his hands on Vega's shoulders and held him there, thinking that was not the smartest move he ever made.

Vega tried to push Alex from him. Something was very wrong. His chest and face hurt like hell. Normally he would have dispensed with Alex. This time he could not.

"Donna has gone for your son and Mac...Mr. Vega, **please**..." and Alex's voice trailed off as he tightened his grip on Vega.

Mac burst through the door along with Donna and Pauli, one man to each side of the bed and they too helped to subdue their boss. Donna stood there watching. Her interest in him had never subsided, even though she had been Marc's girlfriend for years. It had kept her in the Vega household...near Philip.

By now JJ was terrified and she backed towards the open door. Out of the side of his eye, Mac could see her. Pauli blocked her path out of the room.

"You going somewhere, JJ? I am sure Mr. Vega would like to meet his new nurse. Please come over here where he can see you."

JJ had no choice but to do as she was asked and she stepped forward… and it was then that Mac grabbed her by the arm propelling her into Philip's view. His grip didn't slacken on Vega and his other hand never let go of JJ.

Philip Vega blinked his eyes. He could see the girl with the brown hair clearer now. She had brown eyes like his. But that was all. She looked terrified, with Mac having a firm hold on her.

"What is she doing here? Why do I need a nurse?" And he tried to move his other arm. It lay there not wanting to do what his brain was telling it to do. "And what are all these bandages for…" And then it seemed his brain kicked into gear. "Emma… they took Emma didn't they? While I lay there on the floor…I remember someone hitting me with a bar of some kind. Then drugs…and Marc laughing. I let her down, Mac. The only woman I ever really loved. I let her down!" and he stopped like the whole nightmare came flooding back to him and his expression changed to one of horror. "I shot myself, didn't I?"

"Yes," stated Mac. "You tried to kill yourself, Sir…" and Mac stared at Vega and he watched as Philip turned his head away.

"And Emma? Did you find her? Is she safe?" Philip couldn't imagine life without Emma.

Mac dreaded replying to him. Hell hath no furry. "No, Mr. Vega, not yet…"

Philip tried to sit up. Mac helped him and watched the look on Philip Vega's face.

"If she has not been found, why are you all standing here? And most of all, what is she doing here?" And Philip pointed at the girl, his voice low and his temper ultra mean.

"She's your nurse, Boss…" Mac didn't get to finish.

"Nurse she may be," and he looked at JJ…. "What in God's name are you doing here?"

"You know her, Boss?" All his suspicions coming to bear fruit, and Mac thought if Philip could have got to her, he would have killed her himself. Mac glared at the girl. He knew her, yet he didn't.

"Of course I know her…she's my God damn daughter!"

Chapter 7

A pin dropped and bounced across the floor. Mac was trying to hold Philip both upright in the bed and still at the same time. Alex was on the other side of his boss. He grabbed Vega's arm as he tried to move some more.

"She's your what, Boss?" asked Mac looking from one to another. "I know we knew her, but *your daughter*, seriously…?"

"Yeah, she is…" and Philip blinked his eyes.

"Mr. Vega, Sir… are you sure? You have had a lot of drugs…"

"What are you suggesting, Alex? That I'm high… or crazy? Of course I'm God damn sure! I ought to know! She knows, too. Ask her…"

Mac turned his attentions to the girl. "Are you his daughter?"

"Of course not…he is delirious… all those drugs… too much for him…" JJ tried to get out of the situation, but was failing, her face turning ashen.

Mac turned back to look at Philip. "You sure? I mean we checked her out thoroughly before she came here." But Mac knew deep down that Vega was telling the truth. He knew he had seen her before but did not know where. He tried again. "You sure she was not a former, er, *girlfriend*?" and he used the term very loosely.

Philip was silent. They didn't believe him and if he was honest he could not blame them. They had never met her and they also didn't know he had a twenty-six-year-old daughter, and neither did he till several years ago. And the meeting was arranged and that's why Mac thought he had seen her before. He had…and her mother. But the

23

arrangement had been for the mother and the girl to continue their life away from the Vega family and that line of business. Vega paid... for everything for the pair and the girl took her mother's name...and now she was back. His sons did not know and certainly Emma didn't. He had never been sure how to tell her. That brought him back to reality. Emma. How he wanted her right now. He thought she was dead and now he knew she wasn't. And that's the way it had to stay. She had to stay alive at any cost.

"Jillie... tell them who you are... and maybe... what you are really doing here."

Vega knew her name. No one had told him. Now Mac knew his boss did know who she was.

"So, JJ...Jillie, you have something to tell us?" and Mac's grip on her arm tightened. "Possibly the real reason you are here?"

It was right at that second that the bedroom door swung open and Patrick entered, having been called back to the house from his meeting. The first thing his eyes saw were his father attempting to sit up.

"Sir, Dad, you are awake...oh, my God..." and Patrick's emotions almost overcame him. He rushed to the side of the bed, almost pushing Alex out of the way. Patrick had never been so glad to see his father.

Philip extended his good arm to his son. The right arm was not quite as accommodating and still rested in Mac's grasp. Alex dropped pillows behind his boss allowing him to sit up with more ease and comfort.

Patrick looked up at JJ and then to the situation in hand with Mac's other hand on her arm. "What happened in here?"

Mac looked to Vega. Wasn't his place to say.

Vega took a big breath. Pain shot through him again and they all saw his reaction to it. But to offer him more morphine now was not a wise thing to do.

"Patrick... there is something I have to tell you about Jillie..." He didn't quite know how to start.

"Boss. You think now is the right time?"

"There's a right time?" and Philip looked at Mac like he was nuts. He turned slowly to his son and heir. "Patrick... right after you were born," God, he was saying this in front of the whole household, "I had a one night stand. I never told your mother, in fact I never told anyone other than Pauli, and especially not Emma. And it must not leave this room."

Rossi, Alex and Mac all nodded their heads. Patrick bowed his also but he wasn't so sure he wanted to know. Mac's grip on JJ increased and she nodded yes. Donna didn't do anything.

"Patrick… this is your half-sister, Jillie Jennings. She is… my daughter," and it was like Philip had removed a burden he had been carrying for years.

Philip waited for the outburst from his son. He didn't get one. Patrick just stared at him. His father had lied to him about affairs, to his mother and mostly Emma, but he was still his father and he was still the Don.

A word reached Patrick's lips. "Why?"

"I was drunk…hardly an excuse but I was. I just couldn't tell anyone because I didn't know till a few years ago, and then it was too late. A daughter just pops up one day. At first I thought someone was trying to blackmail me. So we did a DNA. She definitely is my daughter. All I can say to you, Patrick…is I am sorry. After that night I was loyal to your mother till after the twins…and then came Emma." Philip's voice cracked. "And there has been no one else since her and never will be. She is all I want!" He stopped, barely able to control his emotions.

It was obvious the man was in pain but he didn't make a sound in that regard. "Patrick you have to find her, no matter what the cost… I think that Jillie here might be a good place to start. She has to be working with someone."

Jillie cringed. She was there under duress. If she gave them up now, her family was dead… family meaning her mother, step-father and her baby brother. And she herself would never see daylight again.

"Jillie…" and Mac let go of Philip and moved her right in front of his boss. He wasn't gentle. "Mr. Vega…er, your father, wants to know why you are here, except for the obvious reason of spying?" The thought just occurred to him… "And how did you know he was your father? Who told you?"

It was then she pitched in, feeling there was nothing left to lose... and she leaned closer to her father.

"I was there the day you met with my mother. I was hiding in the back room, heard what you two said before she brought me out and introduced you as her friend. I was younger... not stupid. I saw the way she looked at you. Like the sun shone out of you. I always wondered growing up why there was no father like the other kids had. Mom is blonde and blue-eyed. Look at me! I have your coloring... not your looks but dark brown hair and brown eyes, just like you! We struggled for money all those years until she contacted you and she only did because we were desperate. That's why she married my step-father, to give me a home and then Jimmy came along. Poor kid. He was right in the middle of it. Not like your sons and little girl, who have everything they want here. Then I met a guy named Vinnie a few months ago," and she stopped dead in midsentence, emotions running sky high.

"You met Vinnie, Vinnie from Vegas... that Vinnie?" asked Mac, being not so gentle with her now, his grip tightening.

"Let her finish," stated Vega. He felt she had that right.

"Yes. Treated me nice... to start with. I'm not sure how your name came up. But it did. Somehow he found out that we were related." She paused. She really didn't know. "And he wanted revenge. Said you killed his brother...did you? Is that what you do? Kill people? Like you are killing my family right now?"

Vega shifted on his arm to get a better position. "Yes. I do. Vinnie's brother shot and killed a friend of mine in front of me...so I raised the gun I was carrying and blew him away! Answer your question?"

Chapter 8

JJ suddenly found a new respect for Vega, one that wasn't there a moment ago. "Yes, Sir," and Jillie took a step back. Now she knew what Philip Vega was. Vinnie had told her, but she hadn't believed it. Now she did. Vega, after all, was her father.

"Jillie, there are some things you should hear from me and no one else, but not today. And there are things you need to tell me, like where they are holding your mother and the rest of your family..." He didn't get to finish.

She interrupted him. "I don't know where they are," she blurted out, her face pinched and her arm aching from Mac's grip on her. "Vinnie just took them away in a car. Said they would be safe as long as I did what I was told."

Vega hesitated then asked the question. "Did you sleep with him?" asked Philip, so matter of fact, and as he did he looked at Donna who had been standing listening to all this. She had not moved an inch.

For Donna all the bad memories came flooding back to her. The endless nights of Vinnie and then Marc in her bed, hardly letting her sleep, and the baby that she carried inside of her; Vinnie's baby, not Marc's. It had been said Marc could not have children. A baby that was due any time of the day now. Philip had told her she could stay at the house and Emma had agreed.

Jillie saw Philip look at Donna. None of the people in the room missed it. "Yes..." and her voice trailed off. "Vinnie had boasted the last few days of a girl that was carrying his baby... And a baby that he intended to find."

"Let me say right now, in front of everyone." Again Vega looked at Donna and this time he smiled at her. "If Vinnie comes anywhere near here for any reason, he is dead! If I find out that he has my wife, I will kill him with my bare hands. Both him and Marc." He turned his face to look at JJ. "I trust you met Marc?"

"Only once…he came to the house with Vinnie. Didn't like him too much. But it wasn't so much Marc as the man who came with them. Someone by the name of Santori…" She didn't get to finish.

"Santori?" and Mac looked at his boss. "What the fuck is he doing with those two idiots?" He didn't care there were women in the room.

"Don't know. But we do need to find out," and Philip tried to sit up more and pushed the covers back.

"Boss, you only just woke up. You have to stay there at least till the I.V comes out…" Alex pleaded.

"Dad, Alex is right. Jillie isn't going anywhere tonight, except to her room, under guard. You need to rest…"

"I have done enough fucking resting," and he grabbed the end of the I.V and ripped it from the back of his hand. Swinging his legs over the side of the bed, he sat there, a man you didn't argue with and one you treated with respect.

Mac let go of Jillie and turned his attentions to Vega. Philip, just clad in sweatpants, was doing his best to stand up. Mac swung his arm under his and Patrick came to the other side of his father. As Vega stood, his long hair fell back to his shoulders and his muscles could quite clearly be seen flexing against the bandages.

This was Jillie's father. One she did not know till tonight. He was head of this household. How much of a head she wasn't sure, but she was slowly getting the picture.

Philip stood up with the help of Mac and his son, and they helped him get into a black silk robe. The room smelled of femininity and of Emma and for a second his mind reeled back a little. Mac saw it.

"You okay, Boss? You need something?" Mac's voice was quiet.

"Yeah, a scotch… and a cigarette…" Philip tried to cover it.

"He can't have either of those…" jumped in JJ.

"And who are you to say that?" Philip came back at her, his eyes looking back in reflections of his own.

"Your nurse!" she all but yelled at him.

Patrick smiled. Like father and apparently like daughter. Somehow he liked JJ. Maybe that's why... because they were half-siblings. He glanced sideways at his father. He knew he was hurting, Patrick always knew how his father felt. He also knew that his father needed his wife back and would go to the ends of the earth to find her and he would help him.

"Sir, why not just sit on the couch for a while. Mac and I will stay here..."

Vega went to say something cryptic to his son and thought better of it. Now wasn't the time. He knew Patrick wanted to talk to him in private, and he also knew how Patrick felt about Emma; yet he knew his son would give his own life for his. That was loyalty.

And Mac was his confidant... even though he had let something happen to Emma. Long time ago he had told Mac he would kill him if anything happened to her. Now was Mac's chance to redeem himself. Between them they would find her. He really had thought she was dead. Now she wasn't.

Vega sat down on the couch and leaned back. He was very tired.

"Alex, you stay in the other room. Ladies, I bid you both good night. Donna," and he called her back to him.

"Sir," and she leaned down near him, her stomach about to pop.

He whispered low. "You are safe here. Vinnie will not take you or your child...and Donna, I've known all these years why you stayed here... because of me." He looked into her eyes. He wasn't angry, or playing her. He was serious. He had known and so had Emma.

Tears rolled Donna's face and she was embarrassed. "You knew?"

"Yes... it's ok, really." Vega leaned towards her. "It's just between you and me. No one else will ever know." And Philip had just lied to her.

Donna did a thing she had never done. She bent as far down as she could and kissed Philip's ring, her tears falling on his hand. Then she turned on her heel and left the room, tears blurring her eyes.

Rossi and Pauli escorted a very surprised JJ out of her father's bedroom and back to her own room. As she went Philip yelled to her.

"Tomorrow, Jillie. You and I will talk... tomorrow," and Vega leaned back as if a big weight was gone from his shoulders.

Mac waited till the door was shut. "Boss, you really should be back in bed. I know what you were doing. But your health is more important. JJ isn't going anywhere. We'll make sure of that."

"She damn well better not. She can lead us to Vinnie and that son-of-a-bitch will lead us to Emma… and Marc," stated Philip.

The hatred for Marc was said with such force that Patrick was a little afraid of what his father would do when he found him. He had a good idea. This was up close and personal and his father would finish this his own way…but he had to find them first.

"Dad…" and Patrick ventured forth. "When you shot yourself…" Patrick had started so he might as well finish. "Whose grave were you at? I didn't look at the headstone when I found you."

There was dead silence and one could cut the air with a knife.

"Why?" asked Philip. "Why do you need to know that?" And Vega did not seem pleased at being questioned, not even by his son.

"Sir, I am sorry. I was just curious…" Patrick had overstepped his mark and he knew it and was about to stand away from the couch.

"Sit down, Patrick; you have a right to know. You are my son and heir." Vega paused and waited while both Mac and Patrick sat on the old leather couch. "The grave belongs…" and again he paused, "to your half- brother. Jillie was one of twins. The baby was Andrea Jennings, who died at birth and Jillie must never know."

Chapter 9

There was a huge gasp from Patrick. He could never have imagined what he was unleashing.

Vega stood up, this time unaided. Mac glanced at Patrick, neither of them sure what to say to him.

Philip crossed the room very slowly and looked in the dresser mirrors. He could see three of himself in the panels. Two shouldn't be there and maybe not even the third one. His hair hung low, still jet black, and the moustache and stubble on his face needing grooming. Glaring right at him was the bandage on his right cheek and he reached up with his left hand and pulled it off his face. It stung. Underneath was a scar, a pretty big one. Red and raw. Philip turned his head sideward. Instead of it hurting his features, it enhanced them, making him even more attractive if anything. He flexed his right hand, more feeling coming back now and Philip thanked his god for that. A Don without his full strength was not a Don... in his eyes. He pulled his robe just slightly down from his shoulder and now could quite clearly see the bandages.

"How long?" his voice low and graveled.

"Sir?" answered Mac.

"How long have I been like this?"

"About ten days..." Patrick answered his father, not daring not to.

And all they heard was Vega smack the dresser top with his hand. "And you let me lie there and Emma is still missing?" It was then that Philip ripped the bandages straight from his body; whether he was healed or not didn't matter. He wanted them gone. Even he was not prepared for the mess a close-up bullet hole had made to his shoulder. What he did hear was Patrick's gasp. He ignored it, and pulled the robe back over his shoulder.

"Doc says it will heal, Boss…" added Mac, and he stood up and walked determinedly to Vega. "We have men in Florida and Vegas covering all the likely places. Now Jillie has given us more info we can follow up on that straight away. We needed you awake, Boss… all of us. You know more about Emma than anyone," and Mac let it go at that.

Vega turned to look at him. "If Marc or Vinnie have her, she will stay alive…if it's just Santori… that's a different thing. Jillie is our best lead. Tomorrow, I will talk to her. Explain what happened with her mother. It's not much good saying sorry for all the years you were poor. They were poor because I didn't know they existed, Jillie anyway. I only found out that Andrea died when Jillie's mother told me. JJ still doesn't know. That's the first time I had seen the little grave. It was hard to deal with. It was tiny…" Philip was choked up. He paused, thinking back. With Emma gone and his thinking she was dead, there had been no point to living, and what better place to die than at the grave of your dead child? He changed the subject. "I wonder what the chances were of JJ meeting Vinnie?"

"I gather he went to the hospital she worked at. That's how they met. Went from there," Mac added. "And that led to other things. Like him finding out about you…"

"Jillie has to be twenty-six closer to twenty-seven maybe. Some where round there. God damn… same as Donna and almost to Emma. My wife and my daughter are virtually the same age. How the hell am I going to explain that to Emma? In fact there are a lot of things I am going to have to think about explaining. Maybe my lifestyle is a rotten way to live. I took her from her country, brought her here. She would be better off without me. Pity I didn't succeed!" Philip rubbed his arm and he thought to himself that he was right.

"Dad, that's crazy talk…Emma is probably somewhere praying to see you again. She is nuts about you…and pregnant with your baby. You think she would leave you?"

"If she has any sense she will…what kind of life did I give her? Living in a mob-related world. That's why I kept Jillie and her mother out of it. Wouldn't blame Emma if she does leave me over this…I wouldn't stay with me. I'm like some God damn male whore… one who couldn't keep his dick in his pants! She would be better off with you, Patrick." Had he said that out loud? By the look on his son's face he had.

Patrick was ashen and very quiet in his reply. "But she doesn't love me, dad. She loves you and she always will, no matter what."

Vega felt like shit. Why in god's name had he blurted that out? "Son, I'm sorry. I didn't mean…" and Philip stopped, putting his hand on Patrick's shoulder. "It's just I love her so much, it actually hurts not to know where she is. If she is even alive and safe and if Marc has touched her."

And there it was… If Marc had touched her. Patrick wondered what would happen if Marc had touched her in any way, let alone the obvious one. Emma was pregnant and if Marc was the cause of her losing that baby, there would be nowhere Marc could hide.

Mac almost felt he was intruding between father and son. But he had always been there for Vega.

"Boss, tomorrow we will get Jillie to take us to her house and show us what happened there, blow by blow. And Mr. Vega, I assure you Emma will be brought back and she will be fine."

"I have your word on that, do I Mac?" Philip raised his head and looked straight at Mac, something haunting him. "Haven't we had this conversation before?"

Mac knew he was right. "Yes, Sir…we did."

"I'm tired and we need an early start…" Vega's face was lined.

"You are not going, Dad. Mac and I will take Jillie to her home. Alex and Rossi, too. We will find out what happened to her family and hopefully that will lead us to Vinnie. We know he was seen in Las Vegas very recently. Depends if Marc is still with him… and also if Santori is involved."

"Patrick, you are not head of this household yet…" and Vega stopped. He felt a little dizzy. Maybe he should let them go tomorrow. "Okay, you go. You find out exactly what is going on. I need…" and Philip turned away from them, ashamed of his own weakness. He needed Emma very badly. He needed her strength, her femininity and her love… and he needed it right now. "I'm going to lie down." And that meant to think.

"I'll come back later, Boss. Just check up on you..." stated Mac a little worried about leaving him.

"Right, that's fine. I can get back into bed on my own. Just leave Alex in the other room for a while," and Philip left them.

Patrick waited till his father was in bed and then he and Mac left him. In the other room, Patrick turned to Mac. "He is not handling this well. He thinks he is, but he's not. He blames himself for Emma and everything she is going through." He sported a worried look.

"Do you blame him, Patrick?" Mac was thinking it so he asked him.

"No. I would have done just what my father did. Brought her here, married her and loved her and tried to kill myself if I thought I had lost her."

Mac raised his eyebrows. Like father like son. Mac also knew that Patrick would search with his father until she was found...one way or another.

Chapter 10

Vega waited till they had closed the door before he lay back in bed. He picked up his cell from the bedside table and punched in a number he knew by heart.

"Charlie... Philip Vega. Need to see you tomorrow. I'll leave word at the gate to let you in. About noon. Okay." Philip hung up the call. He lay back looking at the ceiling. Hard to believe he had been out of it for ten days. It was then he realized how hungry he was. His appetite could wait till breakfast. A drink? That was a different thing. "Alex," he yelled.

Alex appeared in less than ten seconds flat. "Sir."

"Scotch and no rocks."

"Mr. Vega. You think that's a good idea? You haven't eaten for days..."

"You my mother now? Scotch..." and Philip's voice got louder.

"Okay. You're the boss." Alex was thinking the boss was back with a vengeance.

"Tomorrow, while they are out. You stay here. I have something for you to do. You don't tell anyone else. You understand?" Determination written on his face.

"Yes, Sir." There was confusion on Alex's face. Why him?

"You, and only you, will go to the gate just before noon and let in a friend of mine. You don't tell the guards who he is and you don't tell anyone else he was here. You bring him straight to this suite. Get it?"

"Yes, Mr. Vega," and Alex handed his boss the drink.

The drinks cabinet was always full and extremely close to the bed. It was gone all in one go and Vega handed it back for one more. Alex dare not disobey him. That one went down as fast.

"Thanks, Alex. Remember tomorrow and say nothing to anyone."

"Yes, Sir," and Alex turned to leave.

"If you see Mac, tell him not to come back in tonight. I'm fine. Just need to rest and think. And Alex, thanks for the drinks." Philip lay back in the bed and turned his back on his bodyguard.

Alex wasn't quite sure what was going on, only that for some reason his boss had entrusted him with this task, and he had no clue whom he was supposed to meet.

Back in the room Philip tried to sleep, but it would not come. Half the night passed before he finally dozed and then his dreams were fitful. All he could see was Emma and each time he reached out for her she was gone. At last it was daybreak, and he was relieved. He was aware of someone was knocking on his door.

"Yeah…"

"Boss, it's me Mac…"

"Come in," and Philip sat himself up in bed pushing the pillows behind his shoulder.

"Brought you some breakfast. Thought you might be hungry." He purposely ignored the empty scotch glass sitting on the bedside table, and set the food tray full of steaming ham and eggs down on the side of the bed.

Vega saw Mac glance at the glass. He was grateful for the food though and ate it down like he had never eaten before; not stopping till it was all gone. Even the orange juice was welcome.

"Doc's in the other room. Wants to take a look at you. Make sure you haven't done anything stupid like pulling off dressings," and Mac cut his eyes at his boss as he picked up the tray from the bed.

"Very fucking funny, Mac. I suppose you told him?" Vega asked, knowing full well Mac had.

"Yep. I did. Don't want the old doc to have a heart attack when he sees his patient running round the room. One who was unconscious yesterday." Mac was blunt and to the point.

"Do I look like I am running round the fucking room? Do I?" Vega's language was more direct than ever. "Sorry, Mac. I haven't slept. All I could think about was Emma. Marc will know she's pregnant. You couldn't really miss it lately. I was hoping for a boy this time…" and his voice trailed off.

A loud banging on the bedroom door disturbed them both.

"Mr. Vega," and Doc's voice could be heard outside. "May I come in?"

"Sure you can," and Philip sat up on the bed and swung his legs out.

As he did so, he moved his pillow. There hiding between two or three large fluffy ones was Philip's favorite .357. Mac did a double take.

"Boss, what is that doing there? You have all of us round you…" Mac didn't finish as the Doc entered, looking extremely surprised to see Vega sitting on the side of the bed.

"Morning, Sir. I thought Mac was joking but I see not. How are you feeling? And let me take a look at that side of yours."

Doc didn't wait for the answer; just moved right in. When he touched Philip's side, it hurt him like hell…but he never flinched. Not even a muscle except to smile.

Mac knew Vega was hurting. He couldn't not be. The Doc knew it too, but to say anything was a not a smart move.

"You won't need me anymore then. You have a nurse here and all your people. No dressings to change and no drugs to give you." He looked up at Mac and he, too, saw the gun. "I should be on my way." Guns always made him nervous.

"Pauli has a check for you. I'll call if I need you, Doc," and as an after thought, "Thank you."

Doc nodded to both Vega and Mac… and hurriedly left. He should have been used to guns being round this family for so long.

"You scared the shit out of him, Boss. And anyway, what is the gun doing under your pillow?"

"None of your damn business, Mac. When you go today, leave Alex behind. Take anyone else you want, even Patrick, but not Alex. Understood?"

"Yes, Sir…any reason for leaving Alex…" yet again Mac didn't finish the sentence.

Vega glared at him.

"Right, Mr. Vega. Leaving in about thirty minutes. When we return did you want to talk to Jillie?"

Vega glanced at his watch. Almost eleven. "Yes, that's okay. I have to talk to her sometime. Can't avoid it. I have to explain to her. Call me when you get to the house and let me know what you find. Call my cell, not the house phone."

Now Mac knew something was going on. Vega never used his cell in the house.

"Boss, are you going out of the house? Please don't do anything we can do for you. Mr. Vega, are you listening? Sir…"

But Mr. Vega wasn't listening. He was looking at his cell where a text had just arrived from Alex. Someone was at the gate asking for him. The 'someone' was stopped there by security and the 'someone' was early by an hour.

Vega moved to the house phone and called the gate. "Let him in. Tell him to drive round the back of the house and tell him to stay there. Someone will meet him," and he hung up the line and texted Alex back. Vega turned to Mac.

"Shouldn't you be going? You need to find out where Jillie's parents are… and you need to find my wife, don't you?" Vega pulled the gun out from under the pillow and tucked it in the back of his sweatpants. He had wanted to shower and now there wasn't time and maybe that wasn't such a good idea to get water on fresh wounds

Grabbing a sweater from the chair, he pulled it over his head. It took time but he did it.

"Boss…please don't do anything that Pauli and I can handle for you." As he spoke he looked out of the window and there passing by was the truck he had seen many times before when Vega wanted something done. Something without his name on it.

The old rusty-red truck with black wheels was the only one like it in Los Angeles. One that belonged to the notorious hit man, Charlie Hill.

Chapter 11

Vega saw the look on Mac's face and turned slightly to see what he was looking at.

"Damn," and Vega knew that Mac would know who it was.

"Boss, isn't that Charlie Hill's old car? Is that why you wanted Alex to stay? To meet him?" Mac wanted to say more, like 'is he going to do what you think we can't'? But he couldn't say that. Vega was his boss and a Don and to say that would be totally disrespecting him.

"Yes, it is. You want to say something about it?" Vega's mood had changed in the flick of a switch, and he looked sideward at Mac, dark eyes staring at him.

"No, Mr. Vega." Mac was unhappy. He was supposed to know everything that was going on with his boss and now he didn't. That was his job.

"Good, now go find my wife before I fire you!" and Vega disappeared into the lavish bathroom that was custom built for him and his wife.

"Damn him," muttered Mac. "What the hell has he got up his sleeve? Hill of all people," and Mac looked round the room. He could hardly blame Vega for bringing in a professional hit man. Wouldn't he have done the same for Emma if she had been his wife? And he knew that Patrick would agree. His phone beeped and he took off out of the room, passing Alex on his way.

"You know what's going down here?" Mac asked Alex, somewhat disgruntled.

"No, Mac. I know about the same as you do. Just to let you know Jillie is by the front door along with Rossi, Pauli and couple of men. Patrick is already outside. Mr. Vega said I was to stay here. Anthony and Mikey are in the library. How's the boss?"

"Good as can be expected." Mac paused. "Watch out for him, Alex," and he was gone.

Alex didn't reply. All Alex knew was to meet someone and bring him in. He hadn't a clue who it was. He banged on Vega's door.

"Mr. Vega…" and opened it gently and looked inside. "Boss?" Alex thought it kind of strange. He hadn't passed him on the way in there. "Sir? Everything okay?"

"Alex, in the bathroom…" and Vega's voice trailed off a little.

Alex opened the door… carefully. Vega was looking in the mirror but seemed to be holding onto the washbasin.

"You okay? Should I get…" Alex was concerned.

"Just close the door behind you. Pain is pretty bad…" and Philip's head was dipped a little so that Alex should not see his face.

"Now or since you woke up?" Now Alex wasn't so dumb.

"Smart man, Alex. Since I woke up. Are there any painkillers anywhere?" His grip became stronger on the basin.

"Doc left some in the other room. I'll get you a couple," and he rushed back into the bedroom. Since he had been with Vega he had never seen him show pain. He knew it had to be bad.

"Boss," and he returned and handed him the pills along with a scotch. He was beginning to know Vega well.

"Thanks. I'll be fine. Just can't let anyone see me like this." He took deep breaths, and then swallowed the pills down with the scotch. Eventually he straightened up. "Our secret, Alex. Bring the pills with you," and Vega moved back into the bedroom with Alex in tow.

"We going somewhere, Boss?" Alex closed the bathroom door behind him.

"Yeah we are. Let me just change pants. Must be some clean jeans round here somewhere. Look in my closet for me would you?"

Alex found a pair, jet black that matched the sweater Philip was wearing, and ones so tight that it was hard to put his gun down the back of them. He pulled on expensive black leather boots.

"Boss, you are supposed to be..."

"Dead? Yeah I know. That's why we are going with Hill..."

"As in Charlie Hill, notorious hit man?"

"Any objections, Alex?"

"No, Sir...Is he driving us?"

"Yes. Problem?" asked Vega sliding on his Rolex.

"No problem, Mr. Vega. Sir, where are we going?"

"To change my coloring. Anyone would know me like this. Only anyone connected to the household and Jillie know I am alive. Better to let them think I am still out of it or even dead for now. It will give them more freedom. Easier for the guys to catch them." Philip glanced in the mirror. "Always wanted to be a blonde... blonde with brown eyes. Maybe blue contacts. Hill knows all the places to go for things like that."

Alex had a feeling that wasn't all Hill would know... that and more. "You sure you are up to this, Mr. Vega?"

"I'm sure. We have to get Emma back and in one piece. She didn't sign on for this, Alex. I think that Marc and Vinnie could be a little sadistic if it came to it. Santori... for sure. Did she see them put drugs in me? I can't remember, Alex. Can't remember much about it. It's blank from the hotel to the grave. Damn it! Why can't I remember?" and Vega smacked both hands down on the dresser. "Did something happen in between? You were there both times. You were the only one that was. You and Mac were at the Biltmore, and you and Patrick at the grave. That much I am sure about. Next thing I wake up here. What happened in between and how did I get to the grave? I know I wanted to die because of Emma, but something must have happened to get me there. Was it the drugs they gave me? Was I supposed to die?"

Alex drew breath. Now he knew why he was asked to stay behind. "Mr. Vega you were supposed to die. Vinnie pumped so much into you that you should have O.D'd but you didn't. You came around pretty quick and knew Emma was gone. You tried to kill Mac, accusing him of being Marc's father. When we stopped you, you took off in your Ferrari before anyone could even catch you. You were flying, Boss. How you didn't kill yourself, I don't know. I, for one, had never seen you so angry. You tried to find her and I guess between that and the drugs all you wanted to do was die. And you tried to kill yourself. We knew you had several guns with you, especially in the car. Patrick and I found you. When the hospital gave you morphine you just zoned out. Been over a week now, almost ten days."

Vega leaned back on the window frame. So now he knew. Alex had blurted out way too much. Some was true and some wasn't. The part about Mac being Marc's father was true. It was all a lot to take in and now was not the time. Now was the time to go meet Charlie Hill and get his makeover started. He planned to go where the others could not go with Hill and that was to find Emma where he thought she might be. He grabbed his leather jacket, left his ID purposely on his desk and ushered Alex out of the door and through the back kitchen to where Hill had his car parked.

No one in the kitchen thought anything of their boss coming that way, and what they didn't know would not hurt them. What they would think strange was when he would arrive home; hopefully if they didn't recognize him then others wouldn't either.

Chapter 12

"Good to see you, Charlie," and Vega did a thing he rarely did. He extended his hand to him.

Charlie Hill reciprocated the gesture, shaking the outstretched hand warmly. There was a bond between the two men, not just one of a Don and a hit man. Hill had come through for Vega several times in the last few years.

"Same to you, Andrea. I am sorry to hear about Emma. I assume that's why you called me?" Charlie's graveled voice some sixty years old sang out in the late morning air.

"Yes. Plus I need you to help me be in disguise for a while. Need to go blonde and change my eye color." Vega zipped up his leather against the chill.

"Why?" was the only word Hill uttered.

"Because I want to be dead for a few days or however long it takes to get her back."

Charlie raised his eyebrows and his voice. "You what? Are you crazy, Andrea? You think you can go undercover or something?"

"No. But I can be someone's soldier!" The statement was so matter-of-fact.

"You? You would want to be giving the orders…I bet even now you have a gun in the back of your jeans…" and then as Vega turned slightly, Hill could quite clearly see the side of his face. "Nasty…They do that?"

"No. I did. I shot myself on purpose." So matter-of-fact, Vega stated it. "You should see the rest of the scars."

43

"She means that much to you?" asked Charlie, knowing she did. Here was a Don that would give his life for his wife.

"Yeah, she does, Charlie. I have to find her and alive, or next time Alex here, and Patrick, won't be able to stop me."

Alex looked shocked. So that was the plan. Find her or die. Vega, that was.

"Mr. Hill," and Alex nodded to him in an expression of 'help-me-out-here'.

"Okay, Andrea, if that's what you want, we can go right now. I assume you want to go in my car?" Hill paused, stroking his white beard and moustache with long sinewy fingers. "Damn, always wanted to drive your Ferrari, but I guess that would be a dead giveaway you are still with us."

"I'll make a deal with you. You find her before my boys do and I'll buy you one just the same as mine!"

Alex gulped. Hill's pay was a Ferrari? Alex thought he might be in the wrong side of the business. A private hit man might be much more lucrative. No boss, but wrong side of the law on your own, and no regular income. Maybe not. Alex liked working for Vega. He was a fair boss and a good and respected one… that's why it was hard to believe that no one had given Marc and Vinnie up. Santori was the only one that probably wouldn't. He and maybe one or two others from Las Vegas.

"You have a deal, Don Andrea," and he stretched his hand out to Vega. Charlie's long grey hair just topped his collar and the beat-up brown jacket and jeans hid the identity of a dangerous and lethal man. Dark-brown expensive leather cowboy boots were the only clue to any amount of wealth he might have. "Let's go. Alex, you ride up front with me and Andrea you stay low in the backseat. Drive is about half an hour. No one will ask questions. Cash only. You'll be a different man when you come home. Not even your little girl will know you. I am assuming it's Marc we are after?"

"And Vinnie…"

"The punk from Vegas? That Vinnie?" as Charlie opened the door for Philip.

"The same. Why?" asked Philip as he climbed into the car and into the back. Somewhere he never sat. It took him a minute, his chest letting him know it was still sore.

"I have a personal score to settle with him. Tell you about it some-time! Okay, then let's go get me a Ferrari, Mr. Vega, and you a wife back," and Hill got behind the steering wheel and after the motor stopped spluttering and coughing, took off back the way he had come at a reasonable speed.

"You okay in the back there, Sir?" asked Alex a little concerned for his boss.

"Fine. Just let's do this," and Philip hunkered down in the back so even the guards at the gate didn't see him.

Charlie Hill had a way with words and he talked most of the way to Malibu Beach. Suddenly the talking stopped and he pulled into a not-so-nice looking store at the end of a long drive. Trees surrounded the place and a couple of gun-toting men stepped out in front of Hill's car, one which stopped very abruptly.

Hill leaned out of the window. "Jonas in? Cash customer."

Obviously the right words and they let him straight through. He stopped the car and Charlie let Alex and Philip out of the car.

"If they offer you guns, buy them. Helps business. I'll get a couple while I'm here. And here comes Jonas now." Charlie said with a smirk on his face.

Both Alex and Philip stared at Jonas. Not what they were expecting. Jonas was a woman and a very attractive one at that.

"That's a woman!" Vega looked her up and down and at the skimpy outfit of cut off jeans and T-shirt top she wore, her long dark hair dancing on her shoulders.

"Trust you to notice that, Andrea! You're a married man. Let's keep it like that, shall we?" and Charlie Hill's laugh was dirty as he smacked Jonas on the backside. She laughed a raucous laugh like she was quite used to that from Hill.

"And you must be Mr. Black," and she turned her attentions to Philip. "Attractive man like you, why on earth would you need my services?" and she laughed again, an infectious kind of laugh that seemed to stem from her inner personality.

"Man needs to change his identity," chimed in Charlie. "Wants to go blonde for a while. Maybe blue eyes. You know completely different look. Just temporarily."

Jonas knew exactly who Vega was but they were paying cash and cash had a way of speaking volumes. One didn't live in this town without knowing who the top mob guys were. "Come this way, Mr. Black. Your *friends* can wait right here. You'll be safe with me." Again she laughed.

Vega wasn't so sure about being safe with her. Not about his fidelity but hers may certainly be in question.

She led him into the rundown looking building that from the outside looked pretty bad. It didn't reflect the inside in the least. A room full of wigs, hair pieces, costumes, lenses, glasses and dye greeted him, and a row of leather chairs.

"Sit down, *Mr. Black*. You want to go blonde or grey? Same length hair maybe pulled back in a pony tail. Shave your face except for a moustache and dye that too plus your eyebrows. Can't do much about the scar but somehow it enhances your features. You are a good looking man, Mr. Ve..." and she almost said his real name.

"You know me? You forget me! If cash isn't enough," and for a second his hand slipped round the back of his jeans.

"It's enough, Sir," and Jonas realized a bad slip might be a dead slip. "I'm sorry." From then on she was all business.

Outside Alex paced. How long did this take? Even Charlie was getting anxious until the door opened. Both of them stared at Vega. There was no way on this planet that anyone was going to recognize the blonde hair tied back in a small ponytail, eyebrows the same color and moustache to match and bright blue eyes staring at them. It altered him completely. She had even toned down his tanned face.

"Boss, have you seen yourself?" asked Alex totally forgetting where he was. "You look more like a Hells Angel than..." He stopped in time.

"Yeah, I have or someone that used to be me! Still think I can't pass for a soldier, Charlie?"

Chapter 13

"**G**ood God, Andrea. There is no resemblance to who you are. I have never seen such a change in anyone." Charlie stood there just staring at his friend. "Yeah, you can pass. How much do we owe you, Jonas?" and Hill was diving into the back of his jeans.

"Man already paid!" stated Jonas, with a grin on her face.

"Yeah, I bet he did," Charlie muttered under his breath. Half joking...half not. He knew of Vega's reputation with women, but that was before Emma.

"So we get going then, Andrea? If you are ready. We can test this out on the way home." He was looking at his friend, and noticed a grimace on his face. "You okay there?"

Alex saw it also and responded immediately. "We should get going," and he moved towards Vega, slipping something into his hand.

Philip gladly took the pills from Alex. He swallowed them down without the benefit of water, almost choking.

Charlie produced a hip flask from his back pocket and handed it to his friend. "Here, try this..."

Philip grabbed it and swallowed a good amount of the grog. He handed it back to Hill. "Let's go," and he made a beeline for the car.

Charlie blew Jonas a kiss and hopped in the driver's seat of the car, promising to see her again soon, as in real soon.

Alex let his boss into the back seat and slid in the front. "You okay, Mr. Vega?'

"Yeah...I'll be fine. Hurts!"

47

"Need to get him home, Mr. Hill." Alex could read the signs on Vega's face. And for his boss to show pain... it was bad.

"What you do, Andrea?" Charlie asked, half turning to look at him.

Obviously Charlie didn't know how bad Vega's wounds were.

"He has a bullet wound from his stomach to his face..." and Alex stopped, maybe had said too much. Somehow he thought not. Hill was their friend.

"Andrea?" and Hill looked through the driving mirror to Vega. "He telling the truth?"

"Yes," and Philip leaned back on the leather, closing his eyes.

"For God's sake, man! Let me and your boys find Emma..." and Charlie's voice trailed off.

"No... ! I have to be there. I let her down... not you, not Alex, not anyone. Me!" and then Vega was silent, for the rest of the trip.

As they pulled into the drive of the Vega estate, Philip hunkered down again in the back of the car. Alex had to talk them in, and at first the guards seemed reluctant to let the car pass.

"Tell them to call Mac, if they are that worried," whispered Vega. "At least they are doing their job."

Mac cleared them in and the old truck came to a halt at the back door of the mansion. Alex glanced at Vega. There really was no resemblance. Change his clothes a little and he could easily be a soldier... one of the guys. Alex led the way, making sure there were few kitchen staff and certainly no one around that could give Philip away. They made it to his bedroom, where he changed clothes into very old jeans and old shirt he used to play with the kids in.

As he buttoned up the shirt, Hill caught side of Vega's side.

"Christ almighty, Andrea, How did you survive that blast?"

"Almost didn't, Charlie. Almost didn't. And right now I wish I hadn't. I need her, Charlie. I love that girl more than life itself. She's pregnant with another baby. My baby. Even more tempting for Marc and his fucking cronies. Find out what you can about Santori. He has hated me for years and if he can back those two against me he will. Last time I heard he was in Las Vegas. Find him and you find the punks. By the way, Charlie. Not sure if you really know, but Mac is Marc's father, not me. Long story and not the time to tell it. Alex, here, knows, and so does Mac, of course... and Emma. She would have heard it that day. She knew he wasn't my son and then that day they took her it came out who was his father, and the same father will end him."

Vega turned away and looked out of the window. Hill cut his eyes to Alex, who returned the look with a nod. So now it was said before the world. Mac was out to top his own son... and these were rules to die by. Rules that had made the Vega dynasty great had been broken, and Mac knew that. Alex also knew that Vega had thought of whacking Mac once or twice but the bond between them was too great. It took two to make Marc a bastard. But it only took one gun to kill him. And Mac would have that job when the time came.

At that moment there was a knock on the suite door.

Philip went to speak and thought better of it and motioned to Alex to find out who it was.

Alex opened the door to find Patrick there. This would be a good test.

"Is my father here?" and Patrick caught sight of Charlie Hill. "Mr. Hill," and Patrick looked taken aback. Mac had mentioned he had seen him but not that he might still be here. "I was looking for..." and Patrick stopped dead. "I'm sorry; I didn't know there was anyone else with you. Do you know where..." and Patrick stared ahead of him. The man was the same build, but blonde with a pony tail. His dress was scruffy and unkempt and when the face turned towards him, he had bright blue eyes and yet there was something about this man he knew immediately. It was the stony look of a desperate man, a man who had lost something. Patrick tried to read the face and couldn't. He could read the two guns sticking from the band of his jeans, and the buttons done up to his throat threw him.

"And you might be?" Patrick asked.

"You don't know, Patrick?" and the voice seemed deeper with a hint of an accent. Then Italian flowed from the tongue and a laugh that Patrick knew well.

"Dad? Really, is that you? My God, what happened to you? I thought you were one of Charlie's guys. Good grief. No one will know you!"

"That's the idea, Son. You find any clues at JJ's house? I have a feeling you didn't. Right?"

"No, Sir...we didn't. The house was cleaned of any trace. All but whitewashed. When they were taken, they really were. I think, between all here in the room," and he glanced at Charlie Hill, "that they may be already..." and Patrick stopped.

"Dead? I think you are right, Patrick. I think they were dead the day they sent her here or even before. And now she must think I am dead. She must not see Philip Vega again till this is over. You must talk to her. Tell her that they moved me to a hospital. Had a relapse, anything. But she must not see me like this."

"Sir," Patrick asked cautiously. "Don't you trust her?"

Philip Vega didn't answer him out loud, just pulled his son to him and whispered quietly in his ear, while Patrick nodded back to him.

Chapter 14

When Mac and Pauli were called into the room, the looks they gave Vega were alarming. They were both visibly shocked at what they saw. The man in front of them was nothing like their boss, neither in looks nor manner. He stood by the window looking into the courtyard in a different time and place. Philip waited till they were all seated.

"I hear that maybe the Jennings family," and Vega paused, "might not be with us. One, I am truly sorry for that, but two, that doesn't bode well for Emma. Only good thing is that we still have JJ. I'm sorry also if that sounds callous, but my wife is the most important thing I have, other than my children. So let's get this straight right now. Emma is my primary concern. When we find Vinnie and Marc," and Philip stared straight at Mac, who was perched on the end of the bed, "Mac you will be personally responsible for Marc. You understand me?"

"Perfectly, Don Andrea," and Mac dipped his head just slightly with the rift bigger than it was before, and a look passing between the two men.

Vega didn't want that, but Mac had been warned if anything happened to Emma he would kill him, and when he found out Marc was Mac's son the feelings only grew. "Alex, you and I will be Mr. Hill's soldiers for the job. Pauli, you and Rossi will stay here and keep everyone safe, and Patrick, to you I entrust my life." Philip paused. That was a big step. If anything happened to Philip the dynasty was then Patrick's.

It was then there was a loud and piercing scream from down the hallway, and a woman's voice yelling for help. Philip knew that the yell belonged to Donna and he shot out of the room ahead of the others.

"Get Jillie. She's a nurse…" and Vega hurried to Donna's room turning the handle and walked straight into her bedroom.

The girl was crouched on the bed screaming. Patrick and Mac were right behind Philip and rushed to help. He sat down on the bed.

"The contractions… how far apart?" Philip pressured her to tell him.

She whispered so low that only he could hear, a blank look on her face towards him.

Jillie came through the door completely ignoring Vega, not even recognizing him, and leaned down next to Donna, totally taking over. Philip moved away from the bed and stood with Mac.

Donna cried softly. There was no one for her as she brought her child into the world.

"Sir, we should leave them…"

"She has no one, Patrick. I'll stay," and Philip moved back to the bed.

Jillie looked at the blonde man standing at the side. "She'll be fine. I have delivered a baby before."

"I don't doubt you have…" Vega was almost sarcastic.

And Donna looked up at him almost as though she knew him, her eyes begging him to stay.

"I'll stay," and Philip took her hand in his and Donna grasped it tightly seeking solace in the man she loved more than anything. It was their secret.

Patrick had had an idea that Donna was in love with his father and that's why she had put up with Marc. What could he say? He was in love with his father's wife. Made him no better.

Donna screamed again and gripped Vega's hand even tighter and Philip wrapped both hands round her hand and hung on tight. He bent his head next to hers and whispered in her ear.

"You're not alone, Donna. Never will be," and a tear ran down his cheek as he clung to her.

Mac and Alex watched. Never had they seen their boss like this. Not ever, not even when he met Emma. Something had stirred his blood and it was more than likely the birth of another child in the house.

Alex wanted to get his boss away from the scene but he had no idea what to call him. He turned to Mac for help.

"What do we call him?" asked Alex tentatively.

"Good point...try Andrea. It's his name and hopefully JJ hasn't heard him called that," Mac replied.

Alex moved across the bedroom to Philip. "Andrea, Mr. Hill needs us for briefing. He wants to leave first thing in the morning. We should grab a bag, get ready. Mac said there was a lead or two today." He was spouting garbage and he knew it and knew Vega would know it, but he had to distract him and get him out of that room.

Philip looked up at Alex like he had gone nuts, and then he happened to glance at JJ. She was staring at him like she knew him yet she didn't.

Right at that second Donna let the final piercing scream and her son entered into the world faster than anyone had anticipated.

"Mr. Andrea... you her new boyfriend or something? You shouldn't be here. Lady needs some privacy," questioned Jillie.

"She needs me! Boyfriend... yeah, I'm her boyfriend." That was a cover no one had thought of so he leaned closer to her and slipped his arm round her shoulders.

JJ half believed him. No man she knew would want to be that close to a woman giving birth unless he cared about her. There was blood, a lot of it, and things that would make men nauseous. The bed was a mess and someone had some cleaning up to do.

Vega picked up on it and Philip held her even closer to him. So busy was JJ with the baby that she didn't notice the looks from Alex to Philip.

"You and I can sleep on the couches in here. Keep her company for a few hours. Mr. Hill will be back for us about eight a.m. right?"

"Sure," replied Alex. "I'll just let the boss know..." and now Alex was covering for Vega not being Vega. This was getting tricky. JJ had to think Philip Vega was either in the hospital or dead.

Jillie finished up with Donna, making her as comfortable as she could and handed her her new baby to hold while she went about her business.

Then Jillie posed a question to Patrick. "May I go see our father?"

Philip froze. Patrick came to the rescue.

"He's asleep. Wasn't feeling so good this afternoon. Doc came in and said the best thing was complete rest. Let him sleep. You can see him tomorrow." '*A tomorrow that isn't coming,*' thought Patrick.

"I'll walk you back to your room, Jillie," offered Mac, "and just check on Mr. Vega before I turn in too." He cut his eyes at Patrick.

"Thank you. Patrick…" and they left the room.

Philip, Alex and Patrick remained with Donna.

"Geez, Dad. That was too close. She almost made you."

"She did. But being Donna's boyfriend would be a good cover. I can't go back to my own room or JJ will see me. Someone better tell Charlie what's happening. Get tomorrow organized, and Patrick, would you get me some clothes? Jeans and a black sweater. Talk about bad timing," and as Philip said that, he felt remorse. The girl lying there with her baby was in a far worse situation than he was.

"Donna. I'm sorry." He leaned down and whispered by her ear. "It's Philip. You know me. I gave you my word you are safe here and you are, but I must go after Emma. You of all people know what it's like to love like that…"

Donna looked up at Philip with her big brown eyes and smiled. Indeed she did know what it was like to love like that and she trusted this man… and would do so for the rest of her life.

Chapter 15

The hands crept round the clock. Three a.m. saw Alex asleep on the couch in Donna's room and Philip in a large comfy wing chair next to her bed. The house was still and quiet now, except for the occasional crying of the new baby. In the light from the window, and the bright moon outside, Philip could see the tiny child wrapped in blankets resting by his mother.

The gentle crying for his mother woke Philip as Donna's need to hold him quieted him. The girl turned in Philip's direction.

He looked at her. "You need anything? Something I can get you? The nurse…anything?"

"Nothing, thank you, Mr.…." and she stopped not sure what she should call him.

"Andrea…name is Andrea. Donna, soon you will hear noises. Don't be alarmed. I have to disappear. Well, the real *Mr. Vega* does. So when you hear sirens, it's for him, not for me. Mr. Vega is about to die. You understand?"

"I think so." She was confused but she knew why he was telling her, so that she might keep the secret. "Sir? Would it be all right with you if I call my baby Andrea after you?"

Philip was shocked. "I would be honored. And don't you ever call me 'Sir' again. For now it's Andrea, and I am your boyfriend. Later when we are all together again, it's Philip," and he smiled at her, a warm and caring smile, one that could be mistaken for more than it was meant to be.

Suddenly all hell let loose. Yelling came from the main Vega bedroom and sirens could be heard coming down the drive to the front door. It was chaos.

"I guess I am dying," as Philip stood up and looked out the window. "Think they overdid it a little bit, but not to worry. If JJ believes it, that's all that counts."

Alex was beside him in a second, gun in hand. "I didn't think they would go this far to kill you!"

"Mac likes to overplay things. Making his wish come true!" stated Vega.

Alex thought that was a strange comment, but he had noticed there was a distance between the two men of late. But Vega was the boss and that was the way it was.

"Pity the poor guy who is in my place. Don't envy him being a dead Don," and Philip laughed rather a strange laugh. "Alex, lock the bedroom door as you go out. Take the key with you so no one else can get in here. Bring my bag with you, my ID and even my passport. Don't leave any personal things like that in there. When you come back, if you can, text me first. I'll let you in... and watch who you talk to out there. Only talk about any of this to Mac and Pauli and of course Patrick. Got it?"

"Yes, Sir..." and Alex left, locking the door after him.

Philip returned to his seat. Donna was dozing, so he took off into her bathroom. It wasn't like his. It was plain and simple, white tiles, regular sink and bath. Everything was regular... that was the problem. Why wasn't his life this simple? He looked into the mirror and turned the light on half beam. A man even he didn't know looked back. No wonder no one had recognized him. He wasn't sure he liked what he saw, and what he saw was a deadly weapon waiting to destroy both Vinnie and Marc. Santori he would take pleasure in. He turned on the tap and washed his face in ice cold water. The same face looked back. Water didn't change it. He was stuck with Andrea for now and maybe for a long time to come.

He heard the key turn in the lock of the bedroom door even from the bathroom and the door quietly close again. Alex whispered his name.

"In here," Philip whispered back.

Alex appeared round the door with packed bag and all the things Philip had asked for.

"Everything okay out there? I noticed the sirens stopped. Where did they take me? Hospital or morgue?"

Alex hesitated. "Morgue. That was Patrick's idea. He thought you would be able to move about now in comfort. But it does make him in charge, which is something he doesn't want... not yet."

"He can do it. He knows what to do and maybe it's time, Alex. Maybe I should step down. When I find Emma," and he said it with a purpose, "she and I and the kids should have a real life, not this one. Maybe go to the Colorado house and live there. Take some of you with me; supervise things from there until Patrick settles into the role. Maybe Donna too and her baby... we will see."

Alex knew that this was taking its toll on his boss. But to stand down and hand it to Patrick now may not be the best idea that Vega ever had.

"Let's get your wife back first, Sir, and then maybe you and your family take a break..."

"Your loyalty has never been in question, Alex. And I appreciate you standing by me, you and other members of the household."

Alex had a feeling Vega didn't mean Mac. Obviously it was to do with Marc. Yet Mac had been with the family for years, way before Philip became the Don and was a trusted soldier.

"You want to talk to your son before we leave and maybe the other children? They must be wondering what the heck is going on, especially the twins. They saw you being taken out in an ambulance presumed dead. Might be an idea just to...?"

"Just to what? Let them know I am leaving them this way? They don't need to see me this way. And Patrick knows what is expected of him. I have taught him well enough. We should leave here soon. Go to Charlie's house, wait there. We'll take the Ferrari. You drive it out of the gates. A low life like me would not be driving my car. I'll take over once we are away from here. Go to his house and play by his rules. You ready?"

"Yes, Sir."

"Good. Just want to say goodbye to Donna and baby Andrea…" and Vega stopped aware that Alex didn't know what the baby's name was.

Alex was visibly shaken. "She named the baby after you? Doesn't a mother normally name a baby boy after its father?" and he stared at his boss.

"Normally. Problem, Alex?" asked Vega.

"No problem, Sir," added Alex with raised eyebrows.

Vega knew it wasn't his child and he really didn't care what the others thought of him now. All he cared about was getting Emma back.

As Alex watched in the half light from the bathroom, he saw a determined and dangerous man leaning over Donna and the new baby. And Philip said his goodbyes not knowing that he would never see her like this again.

Chapter 16

Alex had wanted to drive the car with the plates V1. Now was his chance. They both slid into the car.

"Remember the way to Hill's place?" asked Vega and he pulled his cell phone out to text Charlie. "Drive as fast as you want. We'll leave the car at Charlie's place. Tags are a bit of a giveaway," and he shoveled down another handful of pain pills.

As they drove down through Beverly Hills, it was still semi-dark. Nearing PCH, light began to blossom across the ocean waves.

Philip was on edge. "Pull over! I'll drive. You are too damn slow!"

"Seventy is too slow?" quipped Alex, brushing his brown hair from his eyes.

"That's Emma's kind of speed. She..." and Philip stopped speaking, jumped out ofthe stopped car and made for the driver's side.

Alex slid over and Philip took the wheel, powering up the car from zero to ninety in the same amount of seconds, with Alex holding onto the side of his seat.

Morning announced Vega and Alex's arrival at Charlie Hill's humble abode. Looked more like Fort Knox from the outside and the inside had always looked exactly like a gun store. Charlie was out on his porch, dressed in what resembled army gear and was ready to go, enough guns by his side to start a war.

"Morning, gents," boomed Hill, as the Ferrari screeched to a halt and the driver got out. "Great day for someone to die!" and he laughed an evil laugh.

"Exactly what I was thinking," Alex remarked flippantly, "and the way the boss was driving, I thought it was going to be me."

"Very cute, Alex. He was driving too damn slow, Charlie. Seventy. Who drives at seventy?"

"Not you, my friend, not you. Park the car round the back in the garage. Lock the damn place up when you are done." Charlie always had a way with words, and yelled to Alex.

"We should take my truck… and for you, Andrea, looking like you now do, perhaps a Harley might be better…"

"Really? You have one? Where?" Philip was more excited than a kid at Christmas.

"I was joking, Andrea. How the heck can we protect you on a Harley?" and he raised his hands in mock gesture.

"But I am not Don Andrea or Philip Vega, am I? I am just plain Andrea…Where is it?"

"Out back," and Charlie threw him the keys.

Philip hurried round to the back of the house, forgetting to mention that as a young guy he had a Harley and he used to ride it… a lot. Even then security had a hard job keeping up with him as the Don's son with bikes, women and alcohol.

Suddenly there was a loud revving noise and the sound of the Harley screeching round the corner of the house into the large drive. But Philip didn't stop there. He sped up the driveway and onto the highway, quite possibly doing ninety or more.

"Oh, dear God…" was all Alex could muster. "He's got a death wish. Did you know he's on pain pills?"

"No, I didn't. But he's not going to kill himself. He wants Emma too badly for that. Never thought I would see Andrea settle for just one woman. Sally couldn't hold him, never had a chance. But Emma, she is different. She doesn't have to have a hold. He'll always come back to her."

Alex thought that very profound, and then he remembered Donna and the new baby, and something someone had said about an incident between Vega and her years back. That's why she had named the baby Andrea. She was in love with him, and Philip was letting her down the best way he knew how. He was brought back to reality with the roaring noise in his ears and the sweet sound of the Harley returning with its rider intact.

"Thank God!" exclaimed Alex, and cut his eyes to Charlie. "That can't happen again. We don't want a real 'dead' Don."

"No we don't. We'll take my other car. Not the old red truck. It's as marked as V1 is. Vega always did like fast cars and fast women…" and he stopped. "Except Emma." He turned and looked into Alex's Italian brown eyes. "We have to find her, don't we? I called in a few favors today. She's not in Vegas as I think Andrea thought. But Vinnie is, and Vinnie will open up like a split pea…especially when he has my Browning stuck in his face!" and Charlie pulled the rifle to his side. "Never go anywhere without this. Andrea still has his jet right?"

"Yes, Sir…ready and waiting. But wouldn't that be a little obvious, as he is supposed to be dead?"

"Yeah, might be…we can drive. Let's hope they believe he is dead. It will buy us a few days before 'the funeral'. That's all the time we have now to get her out. You can bet that they will tell Emma he is gone. Hopefully, she doesn't do anything stupid till we find her. Getting her out will be something else." He paused. "Does Andrea trust the girl back at the house?"

"With his life. He has known her a long time."

"Didn't mean Donna. Meant Jillie," and Charlie looked sideward at Alex.

"No. He thinks she is double dealing him as a payback. He also thinks her whole family is dead. But you should talk to him about that, not me."

"I will. But he seems to trust you completely," Charlie was on a fishing trip.

"What makes you think that?" Alex was on his guard.

"Cause normally Mac would be by his side, almost glued to him. But Mac was warned long ago to never let anything happen to her, and Mac also betrayed him nearly thirty years ago…and that Don Andrea would never tolerate!"

Philip climbed off the bike, parked it and tossed the keys back to Charlie. "What you two old ladies chatting about? Look like two mother hens there." As he spoke, he readjusted the gun in the back of his pants. It had moved slightly as he rode the bike. "We should move. I gotta get her home safe and sound. You find anything else out since last night, Charlie?"

"Yeah. I was just telling Alex," and he ignored the icy stare Alex was giving him. "She's not in Vegas, but Vinnie is surrounded by the Valdez family. Vinnie shouldn't be too hard to get to. Surprised they are covering him. Didn't you always get on with those guys?"

"I did and still do. Patrick has had dealings with them of late. Maybe they don't know what Vinnie has done?"

"Could well be. Maybe we should make a call first and ask them… or Patrick could! Why don't you call him and suggest it? Arrange a meeting for me and Alex as in business as usual. Andrea, I meant to ask you. What do they think you died from?"

"A heart attack. They know nothing of me shooting myself over Emma. All the world knows is that she was kidnapped, but not exactly by whom, just that Marc was involved. The rest is *family* business and I hope to God that Patrick is up to this and can handle everything that is about to come his way, including a fight for my territories."

Chapter 17

Philip slept most of the way to Vegas. He agreed the jet was too risky and now he was curled up on the back seat of Hill's other car, a brown sedan that looked more like it came from The Godfather. Charlie didn't drive a whole lot slower than Philip, so sleep was easy to come by for the one passenger, especially after more pain pills and half a bottle of scotch.

"How much further?" asked a drowsy Alex.

"Almost there. You might want to wake your boss up soon. I know one thing; no one followed us. I made sure of that. How many guns you have on you, Alex?"

"Two. The boss has two also. The one you saw and one hidden. And you have how many hidden about the car?" Alex smiled.

"Six… maybe seven. Picked up a couple from Jonas this morning," and Charlie laughed kind of a dirty laugh that Alex understood only too well. "You never driven to Vegas before?"

"No. The boss always flies. I wonder if Mr. Vega let anyone know where we are going?"

"Mr. Vega did…" a sleepy voice answered from the back seat. "Patrick knows…and quit with the Mr. Vega. Andrea from now on. Heard you say we were nearly there, Charlie. If you pass any gas stations, stop would you? Need the john." Philip leaned over the seat to get a better view of the road. "Speaking of which, there is one right there."

"I swear you have all the luck on your side, Andrea."

"Not all the luck, Charlie!" and as the car turned into the gas station and stopped, Philip jumped out of the car.

Dressed all in black and the now blonde hair, he cut one amazing figure. Alex climbed out and followed his boss…just in case. They did what they came to do, and Charlie put gas in the tank, waited till the two men came back and then took his turn at the not-so-clean urinal. Philip and Alex got snacks at the gas station and some for Charlie.

Back on the road saw the clock ticking by. Another six hours of Emma's life had slipped by. Finally they arrived in Vegas, all of them tired and all needing real food.

Charlie pulled over at a low-rent motel, somewhere inconspicuous, surrounded by other buildings of a dubious nature. Hells Angels hung out in the parking lot and between Charlie and Philip they looked like the real deal. Only Alex didn't. He looked like a gangster in his black leather and pants, and with those deep brown eyes and hair.

As Philip passed a couple of the guys on Harleys he commented on the one and passed the time of day with its owner, endearing himself to the surrounding Angels. To them he was a hip guy. They would never have known he was a mob boss.

As Charlie got the keys and opened the motel room door, he commented to Vega, "You are one class act, Andrea. You have them eating out of your hand in two seconds flat. Smart move. Never know when we might need backup."

And Philip pointed his fingers and clicked them like a gun. "Better to have allies in this business," and he flung his bag on the cover that passed for a duvet. He glanced around. Probably the worst place he had ever been in his life. But the last place anyone would tail them to. "Where you guys sleeping? Just kidding. We should all stay together. Even I can see that. Good thing there are two singles and a couch." Then Philip got serious at the flip of a switch. "So where do we find Vinnie?" and his tone changed completely. "You got an address or something?" and Philip shifted the gun in the back of his jeans, his apparent restlessness showing.

"Better than that. Have a 'meet' at ten this evening with one of Vinnie's friends. Brought guns for him to buy!" Charlie said as he dropped his overnight bag also.

"How nice of you! I have one he can have, right in his gut!" and Philip patted his boot.

"Andrea, let me do all the talking. Your face won't give you away but your attitude will! We need to find Santori. Find him and you find Marc…and then my friend, when you have Emma back, you can do what the hell you want to them both. But Vinnie is mine. Personal matter and I think you mentioned that Mac will take care of Marc."

"Yeah, if I don't end him first! Mac isn't here is he? So I get first crack at him, don't I?" Vega stated, sliding out of his jacket.

"Boss…" interrupted Alex.

"Something on your mind, Alex?" and Vega cut his eyes sideward at Alex.

"Not a thing. Not one damn thing!" Alex thought this was not a good time to argue and watched his boss head for the bathroom.

Philip slammed the door behind him, and Alex raised his eyebrows to Charlie.

"Does he often change moods like that?" and Charlie pulled his cigarettes out and lit one up with a used packet of hotel matches that sat on the table.

"Lately, yes. He has had a lot on his mind and then all this happened. All the drugs in him aren't helping, but he has to be in pain still. He can't not be." Alex could hear water running. He looked round the room. He had never stayed in a place like this either and could only imagine what his boss was thinking about the place. But it was a good cover with seedy looking curtains, grimy covers for the beds and pillows that looked totally shot. He looked back to Charlie. "I wonder what the kids thought. Patrick had to tell them something. Pip is too young to understand but the twins are old enough to wonder where their father is…" and Alex stopped speaking as the bathroom door opened and Philip came back into the room.

His hair hung down and he looked tired. "More," and he put his hand out to Alex.

"Boss, you can't have any more. You won't be able to quit…"

"Who the fuck is paying your wages?" and Philip glared into Alex's face, his eyes unwavering.

Alex was shocked. Something had happened in those few minutes Philip was in the bathroom. "Let me look at your side," he told his boss.

"What the hell for? It hasn't changed since yesterday!"

"Let me look. Fire me if you wish, but I am still gonna look…" and Alex made a move forward and Charlie shot round the back, dropped his cigarette and took hold of Vega by the arms. He was extremely hard to hold.

Philip struggled but Charlie held on and Alex raised Philip's sweater. His side was red and sore looking and as Alex touched the skin around the stitches, Vega flinched in pain. Charlie could see the wound clearly from the back.

"You damn fool, Andrea. You're gonna kill yourself. Should have taken my advice and let us settle this score for you."

"No one, but no one settles a Vega score for them!!" His tone was vicious. "If I have to kill the three of them myself, I will…and take your hands off me, both of you, NOW!"

Charlie let go in an instant and Alex removed his hands from Philip's body. The explanation was there as to why Philip was in such a bad mood.

He wasn't healed at all, not in body nor mind and now both Charlie and Alex had their hands full. Vega would kill anyone who got in his way, quite possibly including them.

Chapter 18

Charlie had never seen his friend like this. In future he would step lightly. Vega wasn't a Don for nothing.

"Are we ready to go?" asked Philip, his voice never altering.

"Sure…let's hit the road. Mustn't keep the man waiting. If we get lucky, maybe Vinnie will be with him!"

"Wouldn't that be a treat? Alex…" and once more Philip put his hand out to him.

This time Alex handed his boss a couple of pills and he swallowed them down. Even he knew he was getting addicted but he had to be in control…one way or another.

They passed the Hells Angels group again on the way out. This time one of the biker's girls gave more than an admiring glance at Philip and Alex saw her boyfriend look up. Philip smiled and pointed to his ring finger.

"Married, love…" and Philip moved on by to a thumbs up from the burley biker.

In the car no one spoke, but Charlie smiled and noted that his friend, once again, had not lost his touch with women. Might come in useful later on.

Ten p.m. saw the car pull into a parking lot on the very seedy side of Vegas. Charlie dipped the headlights and a car already there did the same.

"Andrea… you stay here. Or at least let me talk to them. I'm trading guns for information. Remember all that counts is your wife…"

Philip nodded, but he climbed out and stood by the door, his arm resting on the roof of the car. Alex followed suit and stood ready and waiting, gun in front of his jeans, just in case Hill needed back up.

Charlie moved forward, taking a couple of high-powered rifles with him and went to meet his informant. Only one lamp and car lights silhouetted the two people talking. Alex could just see two men by the other car, just like their ride. Always safer that way. As he looked closer, one looked familiar and Alex dipped into the shadows. He thought from Vega's angle he might not be able to see the other person. He was right.

But Charlie could and his blood ran cold. It was Vinnie himself. If Vega saw him now it was all over. This wasn't supposed to be how it was. It was supposed to be an informant just telling him where Vinnie was. Something was very wrong. Someone had tipped him off... and the only person that could have done that was someone from the house, someone who had slept with him...Jillie. And all Jillie knew was that Don Andrea was dead. She had seen him go to the morgue, so why would she let Vinnie know anything? Perhaps that was exactly why...she didn't believe Vega was dead. And now was not the time for Don Andrea to show up. Somehow Charlie had to keep him in the car and just talk to this idiot punk in front of him.

"So you want a couple of guns and I want some information. Looking for someone called Vinnie. You know him?" Charlie held the guns dangling like carrots in front of him.

They were eyed carefully. "Know of someone called Vinnie; yeah...depends what you want this Vinnie for?" Punk stood about five ten on a good day, long matted black hair. An apparent drug addict by his weight, tattoos up his arms and Charlie disliked him on sight, simply because he knew Vinnie.

Charlie glanced at the car and it was definitely Vinnie. Vinnie didn't know what Charlie looked like. All Vinnie knew was that he had once beaten up a kid named Hill...Bobby Hill, Charlie's kid brother. Charlie was out for revenge even after all these years and he wasn't about to let Vega get him first!

"He knows where a friend of mine is...Marc Vega. Been looking for him. I owe him some money!" Good job the lights were dim.

"You owe him money?" and the punk laughed. "Never heard of it that way round before. You want to give it me and I'll make sure this Marc gets it?"

Charlie and Philip were going to make sure he got it all right, but not the money!

"Nah, want to give it to him personally. Can you ask Vinnie for me?"

And the punk glanced to the car.

"He's with you? If he is, I can just ask him myself. Maybe he can use the guns..." and Charlie turned to go to the car.

There was a .357 pointing right at him. Punk with no name was right at the side of him, gun at the ready. "Hold it!" and he yelled something in Italian into the car.

Both Vinnie and his associate got out and ambled around to Charlie.

"Boss, trouble! They have Charlie..."

"I see it! Let's go..." and he stopped dead. "Do you see who is with them? Stay here Alex...."

"Won't Vinnie know you?"

"You could see him? My own son didn't know me! Stay here. Have your gun ready and pointed at them."

Vega took off at a good clip across to Charlie. "Anything wrong?"

"Your friend here wants to meet Vinnie..." put in the punk.

"Vinnie?" asked Vega. "We came to find out where he is." Philip pretended to look at both the men. "One of you him?" His eyes lingered just a little longer on Vinnie and he took a step forward.

Charlie saw it. "This punk here was just pointing him out to me," and he looked at Vinnie.

"I'm Vinnie. What do you guys want? You got new guns? But why are you looking for me? Or Marc? I haven't seen him for a few days. I can give him the money next time I see him..." and he reached out for the cash.

"Think I'll give it to him myself. You know where he is?"

"Nope. But wherever he is he is a happy man. Found the love of his life. Took off with her..." and Vinnie, Vinnie from Vegas, looked straight at Vega almost making him. He knew him yet he didn't. This man was blonde; blue eyed and had a scar down his face.

Charlie jumped in. "I know you from somewhere, Vinnie, don't I? Sure I do. You ever heard of Bobby Hill?"

Vinnie froze, pushed his dark hair back and shady brown eyes squinted in the light. "Yeah, some kid from the west coast that I beat up once. Had it coming, little punk…stole from me. Said his brother would never give money for drugs…"

Charlie reached forward and with one clenched fist knocked Vinnie out cold. He went sprawling across the concrete and just missed hitting the front of the car. Immediately the .357 was right in Hill's face. Charlie raised his hands. As instinct had made him, Philip's gun was now sticking in the punk's back, ready to kill if needs be.

And Philip was trying real hard not to do that. The punk dropped his gun hand, and lowered his arm by his side.

"Well, guess he had it coming. Don't hold too much with drugs even though looks like that. Drugs don't get you anywhere. Now guns? Different story. I'll take those as payment for you finding Vinnie. Drugs were his thing." He turned to his friend. "Let's go, they can have him," and he laughed a strange laugh, jumped into the car and pulled away at a speed almost as good as Vega's.

"Unexpected turn of events. We now have a hostage and a damn good one at that. All we have to do is to stop him making you, Andrea, and we will get to Marc and to Emma! Alex, help me get this idiot up from the ground and into the back of the car with you." He paused. "Would you really have fired, Andrea?"

Philip didn't answer him, just climbed into the front seat, knowing indeed he would have.

One thing they had forgotten was Vinnie's connection to Santori. .. And that was Santori was Vinnie's uncle.

Chapter 19

Vinnie lay in a heap on the back seat next to Alex. It became clearer and with good reasoning why Vega had brought Alex and not Mac. No one would know Alex, and they certainly didn't know Charlie, and Philip himself wasn't recognizable. But mostly because Philip didn't think that Mac could end Marc; whereas he could without batting an eyelid. The only one he did have to worry about was Vinnie making him. But if his own son didn't know him, chances were Vinnie would not.

Wasn't far to the motel, and as they arrived back it seemed much quieter. Now past midnight the residents were mostly asleep; even the Angels had dispersed and no one saw the car stop and four people enter the hotel room rather than the three that had left there.

Alex almost pushed Vinnie into the room, someone who was still groggy from the blow and put up no fight. He flopped down on the bed and Alex held him there at gunpoint.

"What's this about? You said you had money for Marc..." and he looked at Charlie. "Then you say I beat up some idiot named Bobby Hill...punk had it coming to him..." and then he paused and his eyes focused more on Charlie as Philip turned up the lights. "You look like him..."and Vinnie stopped dead. "Oh, God...you his brother?"

Charlie glared at him. "I'm his brother!"

Vinnie pissed himself on the bed, and squirmed back along the covers. "You wanted Marc right? I only beat the kid up..." he was getting in deeper.

"That kid, as you call him, died...they said later due to brain injuries from a beating!" Charlie's voice was not quiet.

Philip had never heard this before. Now it was obvious why Charlie wanted to kill Vinnie. Perhaps he should have finished Vinnie himself back at his ex-wife's house and then he and Marc could not have taken Emma. Philip interrupted.

"You like drugs, Vinnie?" and he leaned forward and grabbed Vinnie's arm, rolling up the sleeve at the same time. "I see you do. You got some on you now? Bet you do…cocaine, heroin? Anything will do…"

"Yeah, I do," thinking this Hells Angel just wanted some dope. "Back pocket…" and Vinnie turned himself far enough for Philip to delve into his pocket. "Take what you want, man… It's yours."

"No, Vinnie…it's yours! Wouldn't want to deprive you of it," and Philip took the drugs from Vinnie and laid them out on the table top of the dresser.

Charlie watched him carefully. He knew what his friend was doing. Killing him softly like he had tried to kill him.

"Bring him here." Vega stated.

Alex hauled Vinnie up bodily from the bed.

"You wanna show me how to do drugs, Vinnie? See I never did them at all till a couple weeks ago, when someone introduced them to me, only that was by a needle. But I am told you can snort them up your nose and if you snort too much you die! Isn't that right, Charlie?"

"That's what I was told," Hill replied. "Andrea, let me…"

Too late. Vinnie's nose was buried in the drug, Alex held him down as Philip rubbed his face along the dresser with enough stuff going into his nostrils. Vinnie was choking on the stuff but neither Alex nor Philip flinched. Then as suddenly as it started it stopped as if by a secret command from Vega and Alex raised the kid's head.

"Where is Marc? And better still where is my wife?" Vega glared down at the guy with white powder billowing from his nose and mouth.

Vinnie stared in horror as slowly recognition set in. "You're dead! You're dead! Jillie said…" and he spluttered and chocked on the white powder of destruction, one that had cost so many their lives.

Now Charlie knew he had to kill Vinnie. He could not let Vega do it. He had blown his cover quite intentionally.

"As you can see, I am not dead… but I think in about five more minutes you will be! Where is Marc?" And Philip grabbed hold of him, shaking him, while Vinnie vomited down his chest.

"Florida! He's in Florida with Santori…my uncle, and if you kill me, he will kill the girl. He and Marc are fighting over her," and Vinnie laughed in Vega's face, his eyes wild and desperate. "You should have OD'd that day I fed you dope…pity…" and now Vinnie was out of control.

"Florida where? Miami?" yelled Vega and Alex shoved the gun harder into Vinnie's side.

"Yeah, Miami…and I'm glad! You killed my brother and we took your wife…no, that's not true. Marc *took* your wife…" and the Vinnie put the emphasis on took.

"He did what?" and Vega's voice rose higher.

"She was pregnant, wasn't she?" Vinnie was now going past the point of no return and he had nothing to lose. He knew he was about to die… one way or another, either by OD'ing or by lead poisoning.

"Was?" yelled Vega.

And Vinnie laughed louder and louder, till it was attracting attention from the next room, and someone came to their door to see if all was okay.

"You need any help in there, mate?" yelled the Angel with the best Harley ever.

"No, not right now. Maybe later though," Philip yelled back.

"You got it, partner," and the neighbor left.

"She *was* pregnant? Is that what you said…" Don Andrea's face was screwed in anger.

"Yeah. It wasn't me. I swear! It was Marc. When she wouldn't sleep with him, he beat her about a bit and then she…"

Vega could not listen to anymore. He raised his arm back and hit Vinnie so hard that his head hit the table and blood spurted from a fresh gash on his temple, causing him to slide down towards the floor.

"Andrea! Let me finish him," and Charlie had his gun ready complete with silencer attached.

Vega turned away, sick to his stomach, pain shooting through his chest, and he dashed into the bathroom and threw up in the sink. Alex let go of Vinnie and went after his boss.

Charlie stood there. He felt for a pulse in Vinnie's neck. Nothing. A bullet was not necessary. Don Andrea had ended the punk's life all by himself.

"One down, two to go," whispered Charlie Hill, "and by God Marc, Vinnie had better be lying, or you will be glad to die....you and Jillie."

Chapter 20

In the bathroom Philip grabbed the sink so hard his hands were turning white. He stopped vomiting and looked in the filthy mirror above the cracked bowl. Even he was shocked at what he had done and the violence he had done it with. He instinctively knew that Vinnie was dead. No one had to tell him.

The pain in this chest was excruciating and he thought maybe he was having a heart attack, falling backwards towards the toilet. Alex reached him just in time and he yelled for Charlie.

"Boss, sit down on the chair," and he guided Vega to the chair near the bathtub. "Charlie," he yelled again.

Hill rushed into the room, pushing his gun down the back of his pants.

"I think the boss may be having a heart attack..." he didn't finish.

"I'm fine, really. Fine"

And both men could see he was not.

"I'm calling Patrick," announced Alex. "He needs to know what has gone down and also to keep Jillie under lock and key."

This time Vega didn't disagree. They all needed protection at the house, especially Donna and the baby... quite possibly Vinnie's child. And right now Vega needed his son.

Alex used his cell and even though it was very late, Patrick picked up immediately.

"Patrick, Alex. We met up with Vinnie. Emma is in Miami with Marc and Santori, and I have to tell you, Vinnie is dead. Your father sent him to a better life. And, Patrick, your father needs you with him. I think," Alex paused. "He may be having a heart attack…"

Philip grabbed the phone from Alex. "I am not having a heart attack… I am fine. It's just the bullet wound. My own damn fault," and Vega glared at Alex. "We are going to clean up here, get some rest for a few hours and then drive home. Patrick, I want you to get to Hill's house. Bring Mac with you. Just you two. But make damned sure that Jillie has twenty-four seven guards on her. She's paying me back just like I thought she was. And Donna, have Pauli stay with her and the baby night and day. He is not to leave her. Do not let Jillie near her. You understand?" There was the correct reply from the end of the phone and then came the bombshell. "Patrick…it's Emma. Vinnie said that Emma maybe lost the baby…" and Vega ceased speaking and handed the phone back to Alex.

"Your father is okay but I doubt that Marc will be when he gets to him…and get the jet ready. Have it on stand-by at Santa Monica airport. We'll all be going to Florida. I'll take care of your father, Patrick."

Alex put the cell away. "You need more pills, Boss?"

"Couple," and Vega glanced out of the bathroom.

"We covered Vinnie, Andrea. We need to get him into the car before it's light. People in the next room might give us up to the cops."

"I doubt it. They might be Hells Angels, but even they have a code and they liked my boss," commented Alex. "They may even help us."

"They may, Alex. They certainly won't say anything." Philip turned to Charlie. "I'm sorry, Charlie, about your brother. I really didn't know. If I had, I would have ended Vinnie sooner," and Vega sat down on the bed nearest the bathroom. "Got any scotch?"

Alex knew it was no good arguing with him and passed him the bottle that had been in the car. "Food, Boss?"

"We have food?" asked Philip.

"Twenty-four hour pizza place next door. I can call them or just go there."

"Go there. Charlie is here with me. Get pizza, drinks, chips… anything we can take on the trip back in a few hours." Philip winced. Obviously this was a front for the real feelings behind the mask.

Alex was gone out of the door. He had a feeling Vega wanted to talk to Hill on his own. He was right.

Philip leaned back on the bed and Charlie pushed pillows behind him.

"Charlie, I didn't mean to kill Vinnie. I was so angry that I just snapped…" A Don didn't usually apologize for his actions and didn't have to.

"I know that, Andrea. It was my job to do it. But your anger was justified and I understand. But to earn my Ferrari, you have to let me do the jobs for you."

"Agreed," and Philip stretched his arm to Charlie, his hand wide open.

Charlie shook the hand. "We'll find her, Andrea. We'll get your lady back and you will take her home."

"Home…bitter sweet. I wonder if she will want to go back there." Philip was concerned.

"Why would you think she wouldn't, Andrea? She must love you an awful lot. She left her country and her life for you. Gave you a little girl and most of all entered your world…something most women would not do. You doubt her?" Charlie was confused by his friend's statements.

"Oh, my God, no. I wonder if I am deserving of her and should she be in my world. All I have brought her is misery in the last few weeks, and there are things I have to explain to her, like Jillie and Donna."

"Andrea, I have to ask you. Alex mentioned Donna named her baby after you." He paused dreading the question. "It's not your son, is it?"

Philip looked his friend in the eyes. "Would it make a difference if it was?"

"No, not to me." Loaded answer.

Philip smiled. "No, he is not my son. I have been totally faithful to Emma since the day I brought her to the States. I would and will never cheat on her. On that you have my word. But Donna has loved me for years. I knew and Emma knew. But Jillie is going to be tough to explain to Emma. If she knows I did it once right after I was married…"

"I get your point."

The door to the room opened and Alex appeared with a ton of food, so much he could hardly carry it. Large brown paper bags hung from his arms.

"You eat, boss. Charlie and I will put our friend in the trunk. Then we can eat," and the two went out the door loaded down with a body, leaving the food for Vega.

Philip felt a little better without Vinnie being in the room. It still didn't seem right as to what he had done. He opened the pizza box that Alex had set on the end of the bed. Took a slice and washed it down with the rest of the scotch. He leaned back on the pillow and closed his eyes, totally oblivious to the outside world.

And all the guys outside by the car knew was that suddenly there was a piercing scream from inside their hotel room.

Chapter 21

They locked the trunk of the car and dashed into the room. Vega was sitting bolt upright in bed, gun in his hand, fighting demons. Sweat poured off him.

"Andrea, it's okay."

"Boss, put the gun down. It's Charlie and me. There is no one else here." Alex leaned over the bed and put his hand on the gun, lowering it to a safe position. "Mr. Vega, you were dreaming…"

"Nightmares…" and Philip leaned back again on the pillows.

Charlie could understand the nightmare part. He'd been there himself, and right now with the pills and scotch that his friend was putting away, could understand it more.

"Stay with him. I'll finish up out there!" and Charlie went back outside to make sure the car was locked tight and no one could see anything they shouldn't.

"Boss, you should try to sleep. We need you to be both sober and alert," Alex said, knowing full well Vega could fire him right there and then and he was taking a big risk.

Philip stared at him. By all rights he should fire him, but Alex was right. No more pills and no more scotch. Right!

"Sleep a couple of hours, and then we go. A shower might be good too. You wanna wait by the door, just in case. Think I will go shower right now." Philip handed both guns to Alex, removed his sweater and boots and took himself into the bathroom. There he discarded his jeans and climbed into what passed for a bath with a hand held shower. But it was a shower and one he could use. Warmish water flowed from the shower head and Philip let it run down his hair and body.

The scar tissue stung as soapy suds touched the length of it. It was swollen round the stitches, probably due to the fact that he had ripped the dressings off himself instead of letting a trained person do it.

The water felt good and Vega closed his eyes thinking of all the times he had been in the shower with Emma and they had made love there. He whispered her name. How he wanted her and how he needed her right then. His body ached for her and he leaned against the wall for support. The shower head dropped into the bath, making a clanging noise.

"Everything okay in there, Mr. Vega?" Alex tapped on the door and spoke fairly loudly through the slight crack between the frames.

"Fine," was the only reply that came back, and Vega turned off the water, stepped out and wrapped a towel round his waist. He happened to glance in the mirror. The hair on his head was blonde and the hair on his chest a whole lot darker. He started to laugh. The first time he had done so in a long time. He should remember to wear a button-up shirt or a polo neck from now on.

Alex could hear him laughing as Philip, just clad back in jeans stepped out the bathroom door.

"You could have told me I look like a badger!" stated Philip as he took another look in the mirror in the bedroom.

Charlie returned right at that instant and even he smiled. "Very fetching, Andrea. Should make you even more irresistible to women. I thought Jonas was going to change more hair color than that?"

"So did I...gonna have to remember about this," and Philip donned a high neck sweater from his bag and sat back down on the bed. "You tidied the room up well. No one would know I just..." and Philip paused.

"You gave someone what they deserved," Charlie finished the sentence for him. "Let's eat some of this stuff and get a couple of hours sleep and we'll drive back to my place. I'll take the couch, probably less infested than the beds," and Charlie grabbed some pizza and guzzled down some coke. "Andrea? Aren't you eating?"

"Already did," he smiled at them.

Both the other men noted only one piece was gone. Vega wasn't eating. Drinking yes, eating no.

It was almost three a.m. before anyone fell asleep and then it was only for three hours. Alex slept with one eye open, partly because he was Vega's bodyguard and partly because he had eaten way too much food and now wished he hadn't. Alex wasn't small on a good day and now he wanted to be thinner like Charlie or that he had the build of his boss. As Italian as he was, he was good looking but slightly heavier than was healthy.

Charlie slept as well as could be expected. Philip was restless, but at least he slept until revving Harleys woke them all.

"What the hell time is it?" asked Philip rubbing his eyes. He sat on the side of the bed and pulled his boots on. "God damn those bikes make a noise! But they did kinda cover for us last night. Obviously they didn't call the cops. Think I'll go outside and say goodbye."

This statement prompted Alex into action and he leaped from the bed and also pulled on boots, following his boss with great speed. Charlie noted that Vega tucked his gun down the back of his jeans, but he didn't see the other one. He could see both Alex and Philip outside talking with the Angels and once more admiring the Harleys, and the women admiring Vega. Charlie was thinking it was time to leave now they had done what they came to do. And Charlie was also thinking that Vega had it in mind the whole time to kill Vinnie himself.

He packed up the bags and joined the others outside. Charlie was just as cordial as his friends and made a great display of liking the bikes. He watched Vega. He could switch on and off like a light switch when it suited him.

Now it was time to leave Vegas. Bags in the car, body in the trunk, and three men ready to go home.

This time Philip sat up front with Charlie and for most of the trip stared out of the window, his mind working overtime planning their next move. That's what made him the Don.

The trip home was uneventful. Straight road, fast driving and one pit stop, and they beat Mac and Patrick to Hill's house. Philip was quite obviously irritated by the fact and called Patrick immediately to find out where they were. He wondered down the property a little so the others could not hear him and spoke to his son. He wanted to find out how the situation at home was. How were Donna and the baby? Was Pauli with her non-stop? And where were they holding Jillie? All questions he was demanding answers to. Whose car were they in? And where the hell were they?

As he was still talking to them, the Vega SUV pulled into Hill's driveway, Mac at the wheel. For once Vega was glad to see him and more importantly glad to see his son. He closed his phone and walked back up the path towards the oncoming car.

"Patrick, I am so happy to see you. And Mac..." Mac was an after thought. "You have to do something for me. You have to come with us to Miami to get Emma. Not sure where yet, except she is with Marc and Nick Santori. But, Patrick, you have to go in my place as the Don!" and Philip slid the ring from his finger and handed it to his son. "Mac, Charlie, Alex and I will be there to protect you. I have to go there like Charlie, as a hit man."

Chapter 22

"**I** can't do that, Sir! Dad, don't ask me, please." Patrick stared at his father.

"You have to, Patrick. I'm dead for now, remember? The only one with any authority will be you. They won't let anyone else near Nick Santori. None of these guys." He gestured with hands at the other three men. "They know they are hired guns but they don't know me."

"But they know me. They know I am your son. Marc and I were brothers for over twenty-five years. He's not going to let me in the door!" Patrick was shocked and it showed on his face.

"He might if he thinks I left him money from my will…" Philip added flippantly.

"But you didn't. You sent him packing with a huge check, but packing no less when you found out he wasn't your son!" he was right up in his father's face.

Mac was listening intently. He knew Marc was his son. He wondered if Patrick knew Marc was his son. He found out the answer fast enough.

"All of us here know Mac is…" and he stopped. Maybe Charlie didn't know Mac was Marc's father, and Patrick looked at his father, a blank expression on his face that said it all.

"He knows now…doesn't he, even if he didn't know before…you just told him." Philip wondered if he was right for the job, and he turned away from the watching eyes.

To have to admit that your personal bodyguard was your supposed son's father was one thing. To air it like dirty laundry was another. Yet he really didn't blame either Sally or Mac. He was just as bad back then, probably worse; in fact he knew he was. That wasn't why there was a rift now. Mac had let him down. He had let them get Emma.

"And before you ask the question that someone else asked me… no, Donna's baby is not mine! Oh, and by the way. Marc lied to us all. He can have children. So now we don't know if baby *Andrea* is Vinnie's or Marc's, but one thing is damn sure…he is not mine!"

Mac was stunned and it showed on his face. "How do you know that? How the hell do you know and I don't? Does he know?"

"It was Vinnie that maybe can't have them. Vinnie took the blame so Marc wouldn't be in the line of fire."

"You can't know that…" yelled Mac, his steely blue eyes penetrating Philip's.

"It's true. You can ask *your* son yourself when he begs you for his life!" and it seemed that Vega was enjoying this little game. "Donna told me. She had kept the secret, ashamed of what had gone on."

"And you believed her because she named the baby after you? Is that it?" asked the heated Mac.

"I've known for some time. Think about it. That's one of the reasons that she stayed at the house, Mac. She just gave birth to your grandchild."

"And the other reason?" Mac already knew why.

"She loves me…" Philip admitted it out loud.

"What is she then? Your back up plan? In case Emma doesn't come back?" Mac retorted sarcastically.

"How dare you, Mac! How dare you speak to me like that! Perhaps you should go. You're fired!" Philip yelled at him, his eyes pinpoints of anger.

"You've wanted to do that for months, Don Andrea! After all those years as your servant." And Mac stopped; ashamed he had spoken to Philip Vega in that fashion. Any other Don would have shot him. "I'm sorry. I didn't mean that about Donna." Mac paused again. "I ask forgiveness…I was way out of line." Perhaps he was sorry or perhaps it was because both Alex and Philip had pulled guns on him and Charlie had his ready. Mac kneeled down on the dirt, dirtying his jeans as he did. "Again I ask for your forgiveness. If you do not believe

I am truly sorry, go ahead. Shoot!" and he felt the barrel of the gun on his forehead.

Mac heard the hammer click and closed his eyes, waiting for his life to end. It didn't happen. Mac looked up into Vega's face and their eyes locked as Philip delayed being his executioner. Vega had raised Marc all these years as his own, Mac owed Vega a lot and the Don was giving him the chance to pay it back.

"Get up. Men don't grovel in the dirt begging for their life or begging to be shot. Your promise to me is that when the time comes you take care of your own son…or I will!"

"Yes, Sir…"

Philip turned his back on Mac. "Charlie, we might want to get a DNA sample from Vinnie before you bury him, just in case, and then one from Marc also… or Mac. Like father like son!" and he stuffed his gun down the back of his jeans.

"Yes, Don Andrea," and Charlie had seen the other side of Vega. He was ready to shoot his own man for betrayal. In two days he had seen him take out Vinnie and seriously think about ending Mac… and Alex had been right there with him, an up-and-coming soldier who would do exactly what Vega asked him to do, much like the ones at the house would…Pauli, Rossi, Anthony, any of them. It wasn't for the money they were paid; it was for loyalty and respect they had for this man. And Charlie wondered how Vega was going to handle it with Emma if she had been 'touched'. He shuddered at the thought and prayed to his god she had not been.

He and Alex took the body from the trunk and disappeared with it. Mac and Patrick stayed with Philip.

There was a certain uneasy feeling between Mac and Philip. It was obvious even to Mac that Alex had taken his place. A soldier who had only been with the family for a few years, yet now seemed to be the 'hands on man'. But that was partly his own fault and he knew it. Philip had known since the wedding Marc wasn't his son, but he had suspected it for over twenty years, so what had changed so much? Wasn't a good time to ask.

"You want to take the SUV or your own car, Boss?" asked Mac tentatively.

"You and I will take the Ferrari. Everyone else goes in the SUV. I assume the jet is ready to leave?"

"Always," replied Mac, gaining a little confidence back. "Food and scotch also on board."

"You always know what I want, don't you, Mac?" and Vega's eyes studied Mac. He had loved this man like a brother. Trusted him with his life and still did. And most of all trusted Emma's life to him… and his expression changed.

Patrick saw it. He could read his father like a book. Page by page… the only one that could. His father was a dangerous and violent man. One who would kill at the drop of a hat. But also one who could love a woman and defy heaven and hell to get her back and indeed would take out anyone who got in his way. Nick Santori, well, he could be dealt with on a higher level. Marc was a different story. Marc didn't know it yet, but had only a short time to live. Did he hate the Vega family that much to bring this wrath down on himself or did he love Emma that much to take her that day before Christmas? Patrick knew what it was like to love Emma. He would always love her, but to cross his father was suicidal and not something he had in mind to do. Not now, not ever. His thoughts came back to the present as he heard the Ferrari's engine start up. He was now to be escorted in the SUV to the plane as the new, albeit temporary, Don. Patrick had four men to protect him, and the most dangerous protector of all was his father.

Chapter 23

Philip drove the Ferrari to the airport. Mac didn't hold onto the seat like Alex had. When they spoke to each other it was all business, and the SUV behind them had a hard job keeping up with the Ferrari, even with Charlie at the wheel. Alex and Patrick sat in the back discussing a line of attack with Nick Santori.

It wasn't that far to Santa Monica and Philip pulled into the airport in good time and a fast speed. The silver and gold painted personal jet stood waiting and gleamed in the sunlight. It was one of Vega's personal favorite toys. He slowed down through the gates as the SUV came along side. Philip let Mac speak and after both cars were cleared under the Vega name, Patrick Vega that was: the new Don.

They parked the cars in the private wing of the airport and headed for the plane. Philip had to make sure he stayed in the background and let Patrick take center stage, something he would discover he wasn't so good at.

Once on the jet, power switched back. Vega once more was in control. He sat at the back of the plane and talked tactics mostly with Patrick. Once or twice his voice was raised, and once he called for Alex and the pills. He was seriously trying to cut them out, but the pain was till there and he needed something.

"Dad, is it still that bad?" Patrick asked, sincerely caring.

"Yeah, it is… at least I am taking them with water now." Philip laughed, trying to make light of things. He changed the subject. "So what did you think of the new baby?"

Patrick knew his father could turn it at the flip of the switch, something he could never get the hang of. He more than admired this man. He loved him and would give his life for him.

"He's cute, Dad. Didn't stop crying though last night. I left Pauli with strict instructions to call with any signs of trouble at the house. But he shouldn't have to. There is an army back there."

"Good. We have enough to concern ourselves with. I am more than worried about Emma. If indeed she did lose the baby, did she get medical attention? She is not the toughest of women, mentally yes, but physically no."

"Dad, I think you underestimate your wife. She has spent several years now with you… there for your every need…day and night! She's tough. You just choose to think she depends on you more than she does. Remember when you killed Vinnie's brother, she was there with a gun ready and willing to help you? She's tough, Pop." Patrick had never called his father "Pop" in his life until then.

"You love her very much, don't you, Son? Don't answer. It's obvious to any fool. If anything happens to me, Patrick, give me your word you will marry her!" and Vega's new blue eyes stared his son straight in the face. He leaned back on the luxurious beige leather upholstery and waited for the explosion.

Patrick looked at his father like he was insane. "Marry her?" and his voice was raised so much that the others looked down the plane to see what was going on. "Nothing is going to happen to you and anyway Emma would never marry me. She doesn't love me! Only you and she always will regardless. I think she had proved that to you. Didn't she just take a beating from Marc instead of sleeping with him?" Patrick leaned towards his father, aware others were listening.

"Who told you that? I didn't…" commented Philip, knowing pretty much the answer before he asked it.

"Alex did in the car. I asked about her, and he told me Marc beat her. Vinnie told you before you killed him… and Dad, I would have done the same thing. Vinnie got what he deserved." There was anger in his voice.

"Alex should not have told you that." Vega was not that pleased.

"Why not? I am the new Don, albeit temporarily, but the Don no less and I need to know what's going down before we get off the plane."

Maybe there was hope for the kid yet. Kid? Who was he kidding? He was going on twenty-eight. He himself was married by then with two kids, and one sat before him trying to prove he was the man his father wanted him to be.

"You carrying, Son?"

"Yes, Sir. Two."

Philip had taught him well after all.

"You didn't give me your answer, Patrick. I need to know. Would you marry her and keep her safe... even as a friend?" Philip wasn't giving up that easy.

"As a friend, yes... but I would never ever sleep with her...on that you have my word!" His commitment never faltered.

"Never is a long time, Son... a long time! But thank you for your honesty. Now I can get a little sleep myself," and Vega let the seat slide back and he turned his face to the window and closed his eyes.

"Sir," and Patrick got up from the seat and moved back up the plane and left his father. He called Alex to him and they sat away from Mac and Charlie.

"Alex, is there something I don't know about my father? He is going to be okay, isn't he?" He looked into Alex's eyes. He would know if he was lying.

"Far as I know yes. Did he ask what we all thought he did? Did he ask you to marry Emma if anything happened to him?" Alex was shocked that he even asked Patrick that question.

"Yeah, he did. Something else is wrong, Alex. Something none of us know about. What is he hiding? Have you any idea? Is there some deep dark secret he is keeping from all of us?"

"I think there is, Patrick. I just don't know what. He is drinking much more than usual and then there are the pain pills. The situation with Mac isn't helping, nor is the one at home with Donna and then Jillie showing up as his daughter. I don't think I could handle all that. In Vegas, he was a lethal weapon. Vinnie just happened to be his target. I'm not so sure he will sit back in Miami and let you handle the situation. He has to be in control and when he's not he just can't deal with it."

Patrick looked down the plane. His father appeared to be sleeping, and then he saw his wince. So he was still in pain from the shooting. He watched his father's face more intently. Patrick had the feeling he missed Emma way more than he let on, but he also had the feeling that getting her back would be even harder for him to deal with. He didn't know how to handle it. Maybe if she had lost the baby, they would try for more... and maybe not. Emma was the chink in the Don's chain mail, the one who could bring down the Don and the Vega dynasty. That's why he asked Patrick to marry her if anything happened to him. He was planning on just that! And now Patrick knew what the dark secret was. Vega blamed himself for everything that had gone wrong. Sons and daughters popping up where they shouldn't, and the whole thing was getting out of hand. When Don Andrea shot himself, he knew exactly what he was doing. He had lied to them all, and most of all to himself.

Chapter 24

The flight was over four hours. Most of the time Philip stayed on his own. He fingered his wedding band, having given his other ring to his son. Serious reservations had set in about the plan he had in his head. Mac brought him some food, which he pushed round the plate and hardly touched. The scotch bottle was a different story.

Mac came back to visit. "Andrea, they are worried about you, especially your son. I think he thinks you are going to kill yourself."

Philip raised his eyes slowly and looked into Mac's. "Now why would I do something stupid like that?"

"That's what I said. You wouldn't." But Mac could see Philip's bloodshot eyes, bloodshot from the drink and the supreme tiredness that reigned there. And there was a sadness about Vega that Mac didn't understand. "Boss, is baby Andrea my grandchild? Is Marc the father?" He had to ask.

"Guess we will find out, won't we. We know Marc is your son, so chances are the baby is what I said." Philip answered Mac with his mouth but in his eyes there was something else. He changed the conversation his way, just as he always did. "We'll raise Donna's baby at the house, just like I promised her. It's the least we can all do." He paused to collect his thoughts. "How much longer? Much as I like being in this plane, it would be nice to see the ground."

"Almost there, Boss." How could Vega not like this plane? Rich beige upholstery, a bathroom with a shower, small sleeping quarters and every drink known to mankind on board, plus foods of most description. Sometimes Mac envied his boss, and this was one of them. He didn't envy him the mess his life was in right now. "I'll go make sure everything is good," and Mac left him alone with his thoughts.

The landing was good and darkness had descended on the private airfield outside of Miami. Two black SUV's without tags sat waiting on the runway as the Vega jet taxied to a stop. Mac went out first and was followed by Charlie and then Patrick. Alex and Philip brought up the rear.

Although the whole Vega family was well known to the Miami family that owned the airport, Philip had not been there for years and any chances of him being recognized were very slim. They were all ushered in the waiting SUV's and Patrick was honored in the traditional way. He now wore the ring and that commanded respect, and the Miami family Caroni recognized the new Vega head with the appropriate gestures.   They were driven straight to the Don Caroni house where the old Don was expecting his guests. When they learned what was needed, they were eager to pay back old debts and help the Vega family with anything they wanted, including dealing with Santori, someone they didn't care for too much. He had been trouble for them in the past and now seemed a good opportunity to get him off their backs.

On arrival at the house, they were all ushered straight to meet the Don.

"Don Caroni, I am Patrick Vega, my father's son…"

"And the new Don," and old man Caroni leaned down and kissed the younger man's ring. "We are here for whatever you need. My house is your house for as long as you need it. You have four men with you and you will take as many of my soldiers as needed. Santori is a bad enemy to me and this is my way of making things right for your family and mine. I am deeply sorry to hear of the loss of your father. He was a good and fair man, and his young wife, Emma, we did not know she was here in Miami, or we would certainly have taken steps to find her."

"I know you would, Don Caroni." Patrick was giving him the utmost respect.

"My man will show you to your room. Your soldiers will stay close to you in the next room." Don Caroni gestured with his hand

and it was done. The older man was well respected by his men. Now in his late sixties and with grey hair and deep brown eyes, he still commanded a huge respect.

"Thank you. That is most kind," and Patrick glanced at his father. "I would like Andrea and Mac to be very close to me at all times.

"That can be arranged." Don Caroni looked at Andrea, feeling he had seen him before, but maybe his old eyes were deceiving him. He was sure they were. He continued. "Please, gentleman, take the room next to your Don…" He wasn't sure what to call Patrick, not knowing his second name was Andrea the same as his father. "Dinner is in an hour."

"Thank you, most kind." Patrick stated and now they had a home base and soldiers at their disposal… and an overnight bag each.

They were escorted to their respective rooms. The house was large and airy, and Philip counted at least ten bedrooms on the first floor alone. He and Mac checked out his son's room first and gave it the all clear. Richly furbished with reds and blacks, it was a typical *family* house bedroom…one that had a lot of money running through it… plus it had an adjoining door. Always a good point. Their room not quite as fancy but after the motel room was luxurious to Vega. There were two beds, TV, and a very nice white clinical bathroom.

"You want the bed by the window, Boss…" and Mac stopped. Vega wasn't the boss, not right now anyway. "Sorry, force of habit," and Mac realized his mistake.

Philip glared at him but let it go. "Let's make this a quick visit. We need to get to Santori and find where Marc is."

"Agreed. Your son did a good job downstairs." Mac stated while pulling a clean sweater from his bag.

"He did and I was proud of him. Maybe he should continue when we get home…"

"You are kidding right?" Mac dropped the sweater onto the colorful bedspread.

And Philip didn't answer him. Just took his bag and went into the bathroom.

Mac looked out the widow as he waited for Philip. He also had two guns on him and he knew his boss had. It would be good to be surrounded by so many loyal men, but he had the feeling that tonight or tomorrow they would be out following any leads they could on Santori. They knew where his house was, that wasn't the problem. Getting to meet with him was, and he hoped that Patrick was as competent as Vega was at that kind of meeting. Santori was older and knew all the tricks. If he was aiding Marc, he had a reason for doing so, aside from wanting Emma, and Mac had a feeling they would find that out when they all came face to face. He also wondered if Vega could keep his identity hidden once he saw Santori and more so when he met Marc. Alex had told them that Vega purposely told Vinnie who he was...right before he killed him.

Philip emerged from the bathroom, hair tied tightly back in the ponytail, and jet black clothes covered his body. Mac could see the one gun in the front of his boss's jeans and as Philip turned slightly the other in the back. Mac thought he looked like someone going to a gunfight, and to Philip Vega, that's exactly where he was going.

Chapter 25

A t dinner Patrick sat to the right of Don Caroni. His bodyguards sat at the table, but at the end of it with Andrea at the very end. Once again he hardly ate-- just pushed food around the plate. His mind was on Emma. He glanced up and caught Caroni staring at him like he really did know him and just as The Don was about to say something, when Mac intervened.

"Sir," and he aimed his speech to Patrick, "If it's okay with you, Andrea and I thought we might go look around awhile. Neither of us is tired and I am sure Don Caroni's men can show us to Santori's house."

Vega watched Mac. He couldn't think of things like that, but it wasn't his job to.

"I'll go, too," added Charlie, even though he was tired. He didn't quite trust Mac alone with Vega ... not right now that was.

"You go. I would like to talk to Don Caroni awhile longer. Alex, you stay here with me." Patrick had given an order and it had to be seen to be obeyed.

"Don Caroni, thank you for dinner. My associates and I will be back later," and Mac stood up from the table and dipped his head slightly as did Charlie and Andrea.

Still Philip did not speak, left the table in silence and was the first one out of the door.

"I cannot be around Caroni anymore. I think he made me. He certainly thought he knew me from somewhere. When we get back, I'll go straight to the room. You guys get Patrick," and Philip took off for the nearest SUV that was waiting to take them by Santori's house.

Once inside the car, Philip was much more comfortable. He leaned back on the black leather upholstery. His own black clothes blended in nicely and he waited for the other two men.

With Charlie and Mac safely in the car, they took off with one of Caroni's men, a tall very Italian guy with a glass eye. Vega couldn't help wondering how he got that. He had a scar running down his cheek from it, almost the whole length of his face. It made Philip finger his own scar and he wondered how Emma would react to it. He could grow a beard back and it would hardly be seen. What he couldn't do was grow it now. It would come back dark brown and his hair was blonde. Lots of things seemed to be going through his brain.

"Andrea," commented Mac. "You have enough room there?" and Mac raised his eyebrows at him. He wasn't comfortable calling him Andrea.

"Yeah, thanks. Alex give you anything before we left?" asked Vega.

"Yeah he did. You need them?" asked Mac.

"In a little while, in a little while," and he turned his head and looked out of the window.

Charlie turned slightly in the seat and looked at his friend. In the light of the car, he could see him. A man who really needed his wife and his family, but one who was ready to do battle… with whoever got in his way.

"Estate through those gates," and Caroni's bodyguard pointed to a huge estate with the biggest iron gates Vega had ever seen.

"Good God!" and he was thinking Patrick had his work cut out for him. If Emma was in there, she would be hard to get out. There had to be an army in that place. No wonder no one knew she was there. But why on earth was Santori working with Marc? He didn't need Marc, unless he knew he thought Marc was getting money. But Santori obviously didn't need money. Had to be something else. Santori was known to be into drugs, dealing them… and so were Marc and the former Vinnie. He still wouldn't need them for that. Then it hit him like a ton of bricks had fallen on him. Women. They were trafficking women…young women.

"Stop the car!" Philip demanded.

"What?" asked the Italian driver.

"Stop the fucking car, NOW!" and it took all Vega's strength not to pull his gun right there and then.

The SUV screeched to a stop, and Vega flung the door open, jumping out onto the sidewalk, rage enveloping him.

"Your friend always like that?" asked the driver.

"Mostly...makes him the hotshot he is," and Charlie and Mac followed Vega. "Wait here for us."

Vega had walked up the street a little away from the main gate and from the glaring lights that surrounded the Miami home of Santori.

"Boss, what's wrong? What did you see?" Mac was genuinely concerned.

Vega turned towards him. "It's not what I saw, it's what I know. They are trafficking women here. It's the only possible answer. Obviously Santori doesn't need money and I know he is into drugs big time. Everyone knows that. That's how Vinnie and Marc got them and what Vinnie has been doing for money. But what Marc is doing is ten times worse. He's in with them to trade young women. Miami is the perfect location. My God, he has Emma. It's only because he's in love with her that she is still alive and safe!"

He stopped speaking. How did they know she was alive? They didn't. They needed to get Patrick into Santori's house to find out where she was and how she was, let alone get her back. What Vinnie had told them was crap about the baby. All bullshit. Santori and Marc weren't fighting over her. Santori could have taken her anytime he wanted to. Vinnie had not planned on coming up dead. He had planned on finding out what he could and getting back to Marc, who by now might just be wondering where he was.

"God damn it! I killed our lead! Me and my fucking temper killed the lead we had to Marc." Vega was furious with himself and was attracting some attention from passersby.

Mac tried to grab his arm to calm him down. Bad mistake on Mac's part.

"Get your hands off me, Mac, and don't ever put them there again, or next time there won't be a warning. Patrick isn't the next Don yet!"

Charlie tried intervening.

"Goes for you, too, Charlie Hill…both of you just get the hell away from me, and Mac, if you had been doing your job properly at the Biltmore Hotel, none of this would have happened." Vega didn't even stop for breath. "Leave me here. I'll get back to Caroni's house on my own."

"We can't just leave you, Andrea… if they get their hands on you…" Charlie didn't believe what Vega was saying. You didn't just leave a Don, and one this valuable, out in the middle of the street in Miami.

"Why not, Charlie? He left Emma to Marc. What the fuck is the difference? Now go, before I shoot you both!" and Philip pulled his gun from the back of his pants and stuck it right in Mac's face. "Mac may as well have killed Emma that day. At least we would know what has happened to her. Right now we don't. All we know is that we are standing outside Santori's mansion looking like three fools, while my son is back at the house and Emma is God knows where," and Philip rested his .357 on the side of his face making him an ominous foe and one his men dare not question.

Chapter 26

They did as they were ordered and climbed into the SUV, leaving Vega on the sidewalk.

"Go up the street and park the car. He just wants to weigh up the situation for a few minutes," Charlie lied. He knew they could not leave him there. Tough as Vega was, they could not leave him, and nor did they intend to. But to get around him now was suicidal.

Philip paced up and down and even he knew he didn't want to attract any more attention than he had. What he wanted to do was call home and talk to Pauli. See how Donna was and the baby, too. For some reason Donna was on his mind. He hit speed dial on his cell for Pauli who answered it immediately.

"Yeah, Mr. Vega…how's it going there?"

Philip killed the speaker part on the cell. "It's going. We are here at Santori's place. Jillie is in a safe place still, right?" and Philip filled him in on the details and got details back. When he finished he asked for Donna to be put on the phone, a move that shocked Pauli. "Let her speak freely; you move away from her so she doesn't feel you are listening. You understand?" Vega was fairly sharp in his tone.

He turned around on the sidewalk to make sure no one could hear him. What he had to say was between the two of them. "Donna? Hi, yeah it's me, Philip. How are you feeling? And the baby? Listen, if anyone asks you why you named the baby after me, do not explain anything. You understand? It's no one's business but ours. Couple of them know how you feel about me. Apparently they knew for some time. But that's it. They don't know anything else." He could hear her voice shaking and could imagine the tears falling from her large round eyes, and he felt bad about it. "The baby will be raised with my children. You don't have to worry about that, ever! Donna…I am sorry. I really am. I care about you…don't answer. I know how you feel. You okay?" He could hear her crying, little gentle sobs. He waited. She replied to him very softly into the phone, and he heard her say she loved him. Philip closed his eyes, and blinked hard. "I have to go, sweetheart. Always remember I care. Give Andrea a hug for me. Tell him that I…" and he whispered so low that only she could hear, and he disconnected the call.

Philip stood there not knowing what to do. Now he had let two women down. Both with children. He walked slowly up the road, knowing the SUV was there. No bodyguards worth their salt would leave a Don. As he approached, the car door opened and Mac climbed out without saying a word.

Vega looked into Mac's face giving nothing away, just climbed into the car and leaned back. Too much was going through his mind. As he did his cell rang.

"Yeah," and Vega remembered not to give his name. He listened and then disconnected the call, his face blank and unreadable.

Charlie turned to look from the front seat. Vega's face was completely unreadable. He raised his eyebrows to Mac, who just shook his head. Neither Mac nor Charlie had any idea what was going on.

They drove in total silence back to the house, let in at the gates by security and to the front door. Philip was out of the car first and straight into the house and up to Patrick's room. He didn't even knock and went straight in where Patrick was waiting for his father, along with Alex.

Charlie and Mac went up the stairs together wondering what was going on. As they passed Patrick's door, Alex stepped out and beckoned them into the room. They were not asked to sit.

Vega was sitting on the end of the bed, Patrick next to him.

"While you were all gone Don Caroni found out a few things." Patrick paused, a little unsure of himself. He continued, his eyes more focused on his father than anyone else. "Emma is not in the Santori mansion as first thought. One of Caroni's soldiers has a girlfriend at the house who sometimes tips them off here. Marc has her with him. Apparently when he heard that my father was dead Marc took off immediately thinking now the coast was clear for him… except for me. He knows how I feel about Emma and he thinks I will claim her for my own." Patrick stopped and paced the room a little. It was all too much even for him. God knows what his father was thinking and he glanced at his unreadable face. "Marc knows we will find him one way or another…or rather I will go after him to get Emma. He let it be known at Santori's place that he will exchange Emma for …" and this time he took a deep breath and plowed right in. "For Donna and her baby!"

Vega stood up to his full height and crossed the room to the fireplace. There he pulled out cigarettes and Alex was there instantly with a light. They could see their boss's face as the lighter flickered. There was an anger never shown before. He put the cigarette to his lips and took a long drag.

Charlie went to speak and saw Mac shake his head from side to side. He screwed his face like, 'why not'?

"Dad, we can't just hand them over… Marc will kill the child. He thinks it's Vinnie's, right?" and looked around the room for help from the others.

"No, Patrick. He doesn't think it's Vinnie's child." Vega said in a very low and disturbing voice.

"Marc thinks it's his? Even before a DNA test?" asked Mac. This was his son they were talking about.

Philip wanted to die right there and then on the spot. Marc wanted to exchange Emma, the woman he loved more than anything else in the whole damn world, for Donna and a baby. And how the hell had he found out so fast that *he* was dead? Vinnie said that Jillie had told him. Vinnie hadn't had time to tell anyone else, even Marc. And the guys back in Vegas didn't know him from Adam. Someone else was in on this. Someone he trusted had given the secret away.

"Dad. Sir," and Patrick was trying to reach his father.

Vega squashed the cigarette out between his two fingers, and it dropped into the embers of the fireplace. Ashes to ashes and dust to dust, and he looked at each person in the room. Which one was it? Someone here? Maybe Mac. After all, Marc was his son. Somehow he doubted that. Not Alex. He had nothing to gain and everything to lose. Charlie? He was in it for a Ferrari. He knew it wasn't Patrick. Then who? Not Pauli. He was thinking about that when Patrick's words reached him.

"What are we going to do, Sir?"

"You are staying here, where you are safe. This is something I have to do on my own. Find him and take him out. This is personal. I have to get Emma back."

"We know it's personal, Sir, but you can't do it alone. We will go with you." Mac stopped speaking and looked at Vega. "Who does my son think the father of the baby is?" His brain was working overtime and he had this awful feeling that two and two made four.

"Who the fuck do you think he thinks it is? Me! He thinks Donna's baby is my son!" and suddenly Donna was in grave danger.

Chapter 27

Philip reached for his cell speed dialed Pauli.

"Pauli, take Donna and the baby and get them out of there now! Don't tell anyone where you are going. No one! You know the place we used to go meet girls when we were young? Go there. Wait there till you hear from me and only me! Do not use any land lines. Don't ask me anything else. Just fucking do it. Take your ID and money and leave everything else. You know where I keep cash. Do not use credit cards. Take Emma's car, and remove the tags. Now put Donna on the phone real fast." There was a pause. "Donna, yeah, it's me. Go with Pauli, sweetheart. Donna, listen to me! Do what I tell you to do, okay? Just do it! Go with Pauli. Take the baby and go. You can trust him. Do not trust anyone else. Only Pauli and I will know where you are. Yeah, I trust him with my life. Just do it! And Donna, thank you for naming the baby after me," and Philip heard her say again she loved him. "Yeah, love you, too, baby," and he disconnected the line.

Vega looked up to a room full of staring faces. Mac spoke first. Not so much spoke but yelled.

"He's *your* son? You and Donna? How many children do you have?"

"Now is not the time, Mac. Now is the time to get Marc and get Emma out, before there is no Emma to get out," and Philip was starting for the door to collect his things from his own room.

Patrick looked horrified. "Is he? Dad, is the baby your son? Please tell me you didn't betray Emma?"

"Drop it. Both of you!" yelled Vega, his face creased in anger.

"You told the girl you loved her!" Mac was furious. "We all heard you!"

"I didn't…"

"We all heard, Dad…"

Only Charlie remained calm. "Andrea, I think we should go. I'll help you look for Marc."

Vega looked him in the face. He understood what he was doing and the others didn't.

"I'll come too, Boss," and Alex joined him. He was beginning to see where this was going.

"You are going with him? Are you both insane? He betrayed Emma, the woman he loves…supposed to love…" Mac could hardly contain himself.

Patrick sank down onto the bed. "How could you, Dad? How could you do that to her? To Emma…someone you stole away from her husband…"

"You mean to someone who you are in love with, Patrick? *My* wife? That makes it any better? And I didn't say I had. You all assumed it. I do love Donna…but not in the way you think, but you and Mac just assumed, yet again, I screwed any woman around me, and if I did it's not your fucking business, is it? Just because Jillie is my daughter you naturally think I did it again after Emma…" and Philip threw his hands in the air. It was no good explaining to them, most of all not his son. "I am disappointed in you, Patrick… you most of all. You will never know how much," and he opened the bedroom door and with Alex and Charlie in tow, left the room.

They stopped by the bedrooms to grab their bags and then they were gone on a mission to save Emma. Vega couldn't swap Donna and her baby for Emma. He just couldn't do it, and Emma would not want that. Philip knew that even if he did, Marc would not give up Emma without a fight.

Don Caroni loaned the men a car, even though the hour was very late. He also gave them ideas where to look for Marc now that he wasn't with Santori. But even so, Vega felt Santori could help them.

"I think we should pay Santori a little visit!" Had Philip said that out loud? He thought he had as he glanced in the rear view mirror and could see Alex's face.

"Boss, he is surrounded by men. We could never get through. That was to be your son's job…" and Alex stopped. "Sorry, Boss."

"No, Alex. You are right. It was," and Vega turned the wheel of the car in the direction of Santori's place anyway.

Charlie dropped the maps he was holding onto his lap. "Andrea. It's risky. I know you used to be good at getting in places, but getting out might be harder. And what if we get in? I am thinking you have in mind to take a hostage or two? Can we do that, just three of us?"

"Santori has a daughter that he is very fond of, one who would make a good hostage. In our teens we dated…I believe she is living back there after her divorce. Didn't Caroni say something like that at dinner?"

"He did indeed, Andrea. You listened well. Do you know some way in there that we don't?" replied Charlie, rather impressed that Andrea had taken all this in.

"Yeah the same way I used to get in and out when we dated."

"You had been here before tonight?" asked Alex, just slightly confused.

"Yeah, many times. But to bring that up earlier was not a good idea. So I just didn't say anything. Few things looked different, like the gates. They looked bigger and there were more men on guard. Funny how things look different twenty odd years later. Janine won't even know me… that's his daughter's name. She was very pretty once, but I heard she had become bitter after her divorce. But secret passages never change!"

Andrea Vega never ceased to amaze Charlie Hill. He had lived one man's life and yet another one. He had obviously bedded so many women that it was amazing he could keep count, and yet he could be giving his own life to save both his marriage and his wife. Charlie knew Philip was still in pain. He had seen him take pills from both Mac and Alex, and he thought about Donna. Deep down he knew this man had not betrayed Emma. He just couldn't figure out the connection. Not yet anyway. He'd think on it some more.

Philip pulled the car into a back entrance at Santori's house. Everyone drove black SUV's in the mob. No one would take notice of that, especially as there were no tags.

The group had two advantages. Vega had knowledge of the inside and both he and Alex spoke fluent Italian…and they didn't plan on getting caught. They just planned to kidnap Janine as a hostage, and get Santori on their side. Tell him that Marc had done it. Tell them anything to get Santori's help or at least make him angry enough to turn on Marc and lead Vega's group right to him. That was the plan.

Sometimes plans worked. Sometimes they didn't. This one had to. Emma's life depended on it. And so did Donna's, and so did a tiny baby called Andrea, who had no clue what kind of life he had been born into and who exactly were his parents.

Chapter 28

Pauli took Donna and her baby in Emma's Mercedes and out into the night. The baby was bundled up tight in blankets and Donna put him into the back in the car seat. They took little else with them, few clothes and a lot of money. Pauli was the truest friend Vega had ever had, right from an early age. They had virtually grown up together, same age, both Italian, similar in looks, and Pauli's father had worked for Vega's father. And now he was risking his own life yet again for his boss. As though someone was reading his mind, his cell rang.

He took the call. "Yeah, Boss." Speaker phone on.

"Where are you guys now? Almost there I hope." Vega's phone was on speaker, too.

"Yes, Sir." Pauli glanced at Donna who until the phone rang had been dozing in the warm car, her curly hair resting on the seat. As soon as she heard his voice she was awake.

"Where are you, Philip?" Donna asked him, her tired eyes bleary and her voice low.

"Miami with Alex and Charlie Hill. Pauli will look after you. He won't leave you. I can hear the baby. Is he okay?" Philip was very paternal. He listened harder.

"He was sleeping a little. We are all fine here. Pauli says we are going to a place you love. That's nice. Always wanted to see where you grew up," and she laughed, a happy laugh, almost a hysterical one of someone who was scared to death.

"Donna, I'll get you guys back as soon as I can. This is only temporary. You take care of Andrea and yourself. Pauli, call me when you get there. And, Pauli, guard her and that child with your life!"

"I will… you have my word!" and they were gone.

Vega had stopped the car and leaned on the steering wheel.

"You okay, Sir," asked Alex. Even to him the pieces were becoming clearer.

"Fine. Alex, call the house. Find out who is guarding Jillie. Tell whomever it is to let Anthony take over. I think," and Vega paused, a worried look on his face, "that Rossi has betrayed us. That or it's Nikki. The others have been with me too long. Rossi was always jealous of me... and Rossi knows who Jillie is. He doesn't know that I am not dead. Rossi always thought my deceased brother should have been heir. Would he stoop to having Emma killed and aiding Marc, probably! Make sure Jillie is under lock and key, in the basement if needs be. She must not be able to communicate with anyone. Someone fed info out of the house. And when we find them they are dead! They can't tell anything else because there is no connection." The last sentence was said with venom in his voice.

"Andrea, I always wondered what happened to Damien..." asked Charlie very tentatively.

"I shot him dead!"

Charlie wasn't surprised, not by anything that Vega did. He was as much a killer as he himself was.

Alex didn't flinch. It was done with Mac's gun. "You want to find a way in, Boss?" he asked, his deep brown eyes wide awake and alert even if was getting to be the early hours. He wondered how Vega was still awake. He had had the least sleep of any of them.

"I know where the back door is. Charlie you can't go anywhere near there. You won't pass for a soldier. Alex you go with me. You got both guns?"

"Always, Boss. You?"

"You guys expecting a war in there?" asked Charlie. "You want me to keep the engine running?" He laughed nervously but he was serious.

"Maybe a good idea, Charlie," replied a more than serious Vega. "Ready, Alex?"

And they climbed out of the car, and joined a group of men taking a smoke by the garage. There were so many here that two more went unnoticed, even a blonde one. They chatted, joined in and found out that Janine was indeed at the mansion. Alex turned around to talk to his boss and he found he was gone… and Vega was nowhere in sight. This was not good. If his boss was caught in there and they found out who he was, he was a dead man.

Alex waited with some anticipation for Philip. Ten minutes passed, then twenty. Where the hell was he? Then he heard what sounded like gunfire. One shot then two. Men shouting, and in the mix there a woman's voice.

Alex went to pull his gun, feeling that Vega was in trouble. He should have known better. Running out of the back door came his boss, gun in one hand and a lady in the other.

"Same ole," whispered Alex, and he took off along with Vega for the car.

Charlie was revving the SUV. With doors open, the two men jumped in and the woman followed Philip, almost falling onto him. He pulled her onto his lap and the car took off at great speed through closing gates. They made it by the skin of their teeth and took off speeding up the street. They didn't stop till they reached the outside of town. Pulling into a closed gas station, the SUV stopped, rather screeched to a halt. Charlie turned on the overhead lights.

Janine spoke first. "That was fun. Forgot how much fun we used to have, Andrea. I missed you," and she laughed, tossing her long black hair over her tanned golden body. She hadn't changed much at all. Still slim and pretty even at past forty. "Don't think my father was too happy. Too bad. It's just nice to see you again, whatever the reason." Janine paused. "Philip, I heard about your wife. You must love the girl an awful lot to have married her. You never married any of them after your first wife. I will do anything I can to help you. You were always kind and gentle to me, my first love and lover. I owe you for showing me what love was."

Even Vega was shocked.

Charlie let out a long slow whistle. "Damn, Andrea, you must be one hell of a guy in bed…sorry ma'am," and if he'd had his hat on Charlie would have tipped it.

"Don't apologize on my account. I was there, remember?" and Janine smiled as she remembered. She cleared her throat. "My father won't sit back for long though. So whatever it is you want me to do we better get to it." She looked at him as he held onto her hand. "I hardly recognized you. Wasn't till you kissed me to shut me up that I knew you."

"I knew that would come in handy," Charlie stated with some confidence.

Vega shot him a look and realized he was still holding the gun in his other hand. He pushed it down the back of his jeans.

"All I want from you, Janine, is to tell your father that my guys here have you. My son and my guys, and that we will give you back all in one piece if you tell them where Marc has Emma. Only one slight problem. Your father and the rest of the world think I am dead, and that's the way it has to stay."

The woman nodded her head. "For you, Andrea, I will do it. Your Emma, she means the world to you, doesn't she?" Her light colored eyes looked into his face.

"She does. I would die for her."

"You might just end up doing that my friend!" Charlie whispered under his breath. Vega was in way too deep for a Don.

Chapter 29

Patrick sat in the bedroom talking with Mac. "I thought Dad would have called us by now." He leaned on his hands, and then stood up. He paced. Today Patrick looked older and much more like his father.

"He will, Patrick. I just wish I hadn't accused him of what I did." Mac said out loud what he was thinking.

"Do you really think the baby is his?" Patrick asked from the fireplace.

Mac ran his hands through his hair. "I really don't know. He did tell Jillie he was Donna's boyfriend. I thought that was just to throw Jillie off. His timing is off though. He didn't see Donna again, that I know of, till down here and that was a few months after she got pregnant. What we do know is that they had a fling years ago… or nearly did."

"I was thinking about that. Something doesn't fit. Yet we all heard what he said…" As Patrick said that his cell rang. "It's my father."

"You want me to leave?" asked Mac.

"No stay," and he switched it to speaker phone. "Dad? Mac is here, too. Where are you?" He could hear a woman's voice in the background which didn't make him too happy.

"We are somewhere on the outskirts of Miami. Best right now if you don't know. Charlie and Alex are with me and we have company. Don Santori's daughter, Janine. We kinda kidnapped her. She is willing to tell her father we will let her go when we know where Marc is… and not until. We need to get some sleep, even if it is in the car, and meet you in the morning. You, Patrick, have to go and see Santori. You and Mac. I can't go; neither can Charlie. Maybe Alex should go with you. Patrick, there are some things I have to explain to you, but this is not the time or place." Vega paused. Everyone could hear what he was saying; both ends of the line were on speaker. Philip didn't want any more secret conversations. "Donna is safe for now. Jillie is under lock and key… my daughter or not, she fed information out of the house to Vinnie and someone is aiding her. I think I know who it is. About time I fed him a red herring or two. And don't ask me who it is. So… any questions? And please, spare me the obvious one." Vega stared at the phone waiting for one of them to say something.

It was Mac that spoke first. "Don Andrea, what time should we be ready and where do you want us to meet Alex?" The respect was back from Mac, quite possibly because he knew there was a lady in the car with them.

"It's almost four a.m. now; eight should be fine. Give us time to sleep and an hour to eat. We'll drop Alex at your front gate." And Philip was gone. He leaned back on the seats. "Think we should take my own advice. Sleep. Janine and I will sleep here in the back; you guys make yourself comfortable in the front."

"Like old times, Andrea," and Janine laughed a precocious laugh.

"Not quite, my lady. Not quite," and he smiled at her, pulled her close to him, sliding his arm round her and offering his chest as a pillow where she snuggled down, quite contented.

It was a nice feeling to have a woman in his arms, but it wasn't the right woman, and he knew that. He dozed. They all did. Philip was dreaming…dreaming about Emma. He could see her, smell her, touch her… and he called her name, quiet loudly in fact. It woke them all. He was hugging Janine tightly to him.

"Sorry," and he let go of the hold he had on her. "I was dreaming about Emma…"

"Yeah, we all heard about what! Yep like I said, you must really be great in the sack," Charlie found it amusing and pushed the hair from his eyes and tweaked his moustache and beard with his fingers as though he was brushing them.

For once in his life Philip was embarrassed. He whispered to Janine.

"Yes, you did, Andrea."

"Shit!" and he glanced down. "Don't move, Janine…" and once more whispered in her ear.

"Lucky lady your wife, Andrea. Very lucky!" she commented. "If ever you need a mistress, you know where to find me!" She was not so quiet that she was making a very obvious pass at him, and let her long hair flop intentionally onto him.

He frowned at her. "I don't take mistresses any more. Not since Emma."

"I do believe you are serious, Andrea. You do love her, don't you?"

"I do." Philip changed the subject. "Seems to be lights are coming on in that café across the highway. Let's go eat."

"Good, I'm starving!" pointed out Alex patting his stomach.

"When aren't you, Alex?" Vega added, "Got anything for me?"

Alex fished in his pocket. "No, Mr. Vega. Some back with Mac though."

"That doesn't help me now does it?" and Vega's tone changed once more at the flip of the switch. He wanted more pills and he wanted his wife for more than just sex. That he could get anywhere including the back of this car.

Leaving the parked car by the nearest door, they entered the café. *Truck stop* would have been a better term for it, and the four folks didn't quite fit in with the clientele that seemed to be filing in. Mostly truckers of the overseas kind and ones that spoke more Spanish than anything else. The looks they got were a little threatening, like they should not be there. One woman, one Hells Angel and two more men, one being very Italian, and a very expensive SUV out front. A group they could maybe steal from.

Charlie picked them a table in the corner. Janine used the restroom, one that hadn't been cleaned in years, or so it seemed. Her black cocktail dress looked even more out of place than it did in the car. How she wished she had a sweater or jacket to cover the very revealing neckline. No wonder Andrea had been dreaming about having sex. She fluffed her hair and returned to the table, only to find Charlie and Alex there.

"Where did Andrea go? Restroom?"

"Yep. Say, maybe I should get you a jacket or something from the car. You are attracting some looks…" chimed in Charlie staring openly at her cleavage.

"She can have mine," and Philip slid out of his as he approached the table. Handing it to her he left his back exposed, including the handle of his gun.

"Pistola!" was the only word they heard from behind them. "Turba," and the patrons found a new respect for their visitors. The last thing they wanted to do was attract the attention of the mob, the Italian one that was.

They ordered food. And ate fast. It did smell good though. Scrambled eggs, pancakes, fruit washed down with steaming hot coffee and orange juice that seemed remarkably fresh. This time they all noticed all Philip had was coffee.

"Don't you eat anymore, Boss?" and Alex decided if Vega didn't want it, he would eat it.

"Not hungry and we need to leave. Hope the damn GPS can get us back to Caroni's house. We told Patrick and Mac eight. It's nearly that now. And your father would have been on the phone last night to the cops on his payroll, Janine. They probably have an idea who they are looking for by now. Santori is no fool. He may be older, but no fool."

That seemed to be the cue to go. Vega paid the bill in cash. Nearly everything they did was cash. As he got up to leave, Vega felt the pain again. He was beginning to learn how to control it so that no one noticed, except for one man in the corner of the room, the man who was counting his cash that he made from selling Philip Vega some drugs in the bathroom.

Chapter 30

They made it back to Caroni's house a few minutes past eight a.m. Patrick and Mac were waiting outside in another loaned SUV.

"You want to talk to Patrick before we leave you?" asked Alex, getting his things together.

"Not really. You can fill him in on any details. Tell him to make a point that we, rather you, have his daughter and he can have her back all in one piece if he tells us where Marc is. If it gets out of hand, tell him we know he is trafficking girls..." Vega stopped. His daughter might not know that. "Did you know that?" and he looked Janine square in the eyes.

Janine looked shocked. "My father? He doesn't do that. He has casinos down here. Lots of them just like you do in Los Angeles. That's how he makes money, that and land deals. He has girls over also just like you do...I guess you don't anymore do you? But he doesn't traffic women," and then she stopped to think. There were rather a lot of young women, now that she thought about it, in the last three months she had been home. "He does, doesn't he?" Janine was ashamed.

"I think so... Alex, tell Patrick to ask for a girl... never mind, we'll both go tell him," and they left the one SUV for the other.

She waited till he was well out of earshot. "Mr. Hill, is there something wrong with Andrea? That scar on his face..."

"Bullet wound, ma'am. Why do you ask?" Hill scrunched his eyes at her, wondering how far they could really trust her.

"Because when he was hugging me I could feel him flinch when I leaned on his chest. Andrea never flinches when a woman leans on him and especially not me!"

Charlie raised his eyebrows. "Scar goes all the way to his stomach, ma'am."

"He do that?" She leaned closer to talk quietly to Charlie.

"Good guess. How did you know?"

"When we were dating, or whatever one calls it now days, sleeping together, we sneaked out one night and took my father's car to the nearby woods. We were making out, and he heard something or someone stirring in the bushes. He asked them to stand still, thinking we had been followed. But they didn't stop and he pulled his gun and fired. When he went to look, it was a baby deer that had strayed from its mother. It lay there on the ground, twitching in death, its blood turning the fresh green grass red. He was so upset and angry at the same time. He pulled a knife out of his boot. He always carried one there, probably now it's a gun, and slit the animal's throat. I promptly threw up, but he did a strange thing. He turned the gun on himself and it took me all my strength to stop him from shooting himself in the hand or wherever the gun was pointing. He said even a baby deserved to live. Mr. Hill, is there a child involved here somewhere?"

Charlie Hill now saw both Andrea and Janine in a different light. "Yes, ma'am there is. Emma is carrying their second child and a young girl back at the Vega house just gave birth."

"And Andrea shot himself over Emma, right? He thinks she could be dead?"

Good God, this woman knew him well. "Yes." He couldn't say anymore. She was so accurate.

"Ma'am, may I ask you. Who left?"

"He left me. He could have had any woman he wanted back then, just like he still could if he wanted. He met Sally one summer…" she smiled a gentle smile.

"Did you ever get over him?" Charlie already knew the answer to that. Vega had a hold over women that they could not escape. But only one had a hold on him.

"No, I never did. I married and as you know, divorced. No children with my husband."

That was a strange statement. She saw Hill's face.

"After Andrea left, I slept around a lot…mainly to try to get him out of my system. Those affairs gave me a child, a little girl. My father had her adopted the day she was born. I never even saw her. She was whisked away. I so wanted the child to be Andrea's child…but even though I tried to find her, the tracks were well hidden."

"How old would she be now, Ms. Santori?" Hill had to ask her. She looked so sad and had just confided so much to him.

"Oh, about twenty-seven or so, I guess."

Jillie's age.

"You have no idea where she is, none at all? Nor who adopted her?"

"None at all. I wish to God I did," and tears streamed down her face. "That's why I offered to help Andrea. I know what it's like to love someone like he loves Emma."

Charlie gave her a tissue, his brain working overtime. But Jillie said one child, not two and Jillie said she saw Philip meet her mother and Philip never denied it. What if Jillie's mother just told Andrea there were two children? What if he paid for Jillie and his dead son for all his life and they weren't his? Yet Jillie did look like him to a certain degree, actually a lot like him now that Charlie thought about it.

"How old were you when you gave birth?" He was almost frightened by the answer.

"Late teens. Philip is older than me by several years. After he married Sally, next thing I heard was she pregnant. Didn't surprise me, nor did the next son. I am surprised that more Vega children did not just pop out of the wood work."

"Me too…" and he thought of Emma. "His wife is almost the same age as your daughter would be. He has two younger children and a little girl with Emma. He loves the children. The more the better," and a bell was clanging itself to death in his head, and he stared out of the car window at Vega. How long had he known? How did his friend deal with all this? Was this why he had shot himself? Patrick was his son. There was no doubt of that, and so were the twins and Pip. But Jillie? That was a big question. How did Donna fit in to this equation? The bell clanged louder. And Marc? How long did Vega know Marc wasn't his real son, that Mac was the father? Long enough probably. He realized Janine was talking to him.

"How long have you been friends with Andrea?"

"As long as pay-dirt, ma'am. We go back. When he needs a hit, he calls me. Sometimes even when he doesn't. We'd drink together. Used to whore..." *'Shit, Charlie, that was a smart statement!'*

"It's okay, Mr. Hill. I know Andrea very well. Even with me he had someone else on the side. That's just the way he is and I thought always would be."

"He changed, ma'am, after he met Emma. Went to her native England to claim her from her husband. Love at first sight they say. He even killed her husband to get her."

"That's real love, Charlie Hill, real love. I hope for his sake that he finds Emma alive, because to be honest, next time he fires that gun, you better be watching where he's aiming it at... or he might succeed in killing himself."

And Charlie Hill thought the same.

Chapter 31

Vega finished his instructions to Patrick and returned to the car. He could sense something but wasn't sure what.

"Everything all right in here?" Philip could see Janine had been crying and guessed it had something to do with him. "You should come into Caroni's house. I don't think he will mind for one second. I have a room…" *That I'm sharing with someone,* he thought. "Charlie and I will stay with you," and he helped her out of the SUV and into the house.

"Patrick good on what he is to do?"

"Yep, think so. All we can do is wait. He has Mac and Alex with him. You are good bargaining power, Janine."

Vega was treating her nicely but a little indifferently.

Charlie and Philip escorted her by the back stairs up to the bedroom. Letting her into the room, Charlie pulled his friend back just slightly and closed the door.

"Andrea, please be nice to her. She's still in love with you… That's why she is going along with this. No other reason, not that I know of anyway."

"I know….." but it made him think. Did Charlie suspect something? He was trying to focus on Patrick right now and didn't need his thoughts wondering about his brain on something else. All he wanted was Patrick to find out where Marc was. Marc, Mac's son. Even though he had known for a long time Marc wasn't his son, it wasn't so easy to accept that Mac had beaten him to it.

Charlie tried again. "She ever tell you she had a baby!"

That stopped Vega in his tracks. Philip was speechless. "When?"

"About twenty-six or so years back," replied Charlie looking down at his boot, thinking how dusty they were.

"Really? And you found this out when?" Vega wasn't so happy they had been discussing him behind his back.

"In the car when we were waiting for you. Child would be about Jillie's age. She was adopted at birth. You sure you know who Jillie's mother is?"

"What the fuck are you saying? Jillie and her mother and I had DNA tests done. I also remember the affair. I'm sure! Now let's do what we came here to do," and Vega all but stormed into the room. But it made him wonder what else Charlie was thinking which reminded him he hadn't heard from Pauli. They had to be at their destination now.

As he entered the room, Philip smiled at Janine. Old memories flashed through his brain and he disappeared into the bathroom, the only place he could be on his own. First he pulled the contraband pills from his pocket. He wasn't too sure what they were except the guy in the cafe said they would ease pain. He filled a tumbler full of water and swallowed the pills down, and then he pulled his cell out and made a call.

It rang and rang. Why wasn't Pauli picking up? Philip was worried, but he couldn't stay in the bathroom all day. As he opened the door, he could hear Janine and Charlie speaking quietly. Something was going on, something he wasn't privy to. She was handing him something.

Vega made a loud noise as he came out, making the door creak much louder than it should. Just then his cell rang.

Philip grabbed it. "Yeah. Where the fuck were you, Pauli? I dialed about six times. Oh, well, why didn't Donna answer it for you? Never mind. How is she? And the baby? You all settled in now? You get some food on the way there? Baby things? Is she there?"

Janine thought Andrea was seriously worried about these folks, especially the girl.

She whispered to Charlie. "Is that Pauli with her? I knew him. He would be down here with Andrea. Who's the girl?"

What an excellent question. Who indeed!

"Baby, you feeling okay? I know it's not the best place to be after giving birth, but at least you will be safe there. Pauli's life depends on it!"

"Baby? He just called her Baby..." mouthed Janine, raising her very pretty eyebrows.

"Yeah we know. Can't figure out the relationship either..."

"He only ever called..." and she stopped, knowing he only called women he slept with Baby. "How long has he known her?"

"Years. She was Marc's girlfriend for several years. But he found out Marc wasn't his son over ten years ago, just not who his father was...but still Donna stayed at the house. It's a complicated story and probably one that should only come from Andrea." But it did make Charlie think even more about the whole situation.

"You like the cabin? It was my father's hunting lodge. Small but cozy. How's Andrea? Never mind I can hear him! Okay, tell Pauli I'll call him back when we have news. And you have my cell number. Use it when you need to." Philip was gone. He wasn't even hiding the fact now that he was so interested in her and the child.

Janine realized how much Andrea had changed. He was so much more of a man now than of years ago. Confident and self-assured, and as she already knew, a man who killed people. That he had always been.

He came back into the spotlight. "Either of you hungry? I can get food sent up."

"Aren't you hungry my friend?" Charlie asked knowing he had hardly eaten for days. Just smoking and drinking a lot of scotch.

"Not in the slightest." He even looked good, like the pain had gone, too. Now Hill was suspicious. Alex had told him he didn't have pills in the café; now he was obviously feeling no pain. Charlie knew those signs. "Andrea, how is your wound?"

"Fine, why?" Guilt was written all over his face.

"Shouldn't we check it, to make sure that no infection has set in?"

"Don't see why." He couldn't let Charlie look. It was red and tender but he couldn't feel it right now and Charlie could not see it.

Hill now really wondered what Andrea had taken that he didn't know about. He was a little hyper and even the scotch he had just poured and downed didn't work that fast. But drugs did. Something that Vega despised. He knew Andrea was suspicious and maybe this was not a good time to pursue this. He had a lot on his mind right now; especially that Patrick was in the lion's den and a den that they had not heard from since the other SUV left. But Charlie had to know. He waited till he could get round the back of Vega and slipped up behind him and almost had him by the arms. Philip, even in his present state, was faster.

Philip had his gun pulled from his jeans and spun round holding it to Hill's face.

"You ever do that again, friend or not, and I will shoot you Charlie Hill! On that you have my word!" And Andrea lowered the weapon and pushed it back into his jeans.

Janine clasped her hand to her mouth. This was not the Andrea she loved. This man was a natural born killer.

Chapter 32

In Santori's lair it was apparent he was not a happy man. The cops on his payroll had come up with nothing, and now at the gate Vega's son was asking for an audience. He had to be seen to want this. Santori sat in an oversized leather chair in the library. That's where he conducted most of his business. Santori was older than Philip and Janine was his youngest child. He had sons, three of them all big tough guys and all very Italian, complete with tattoos. Santori modeled himself on Don Corleone, who had long been his hero since The Godfather films. He ruled his house with an iron fist and his business affairs even more so. He was indeed trafficking in young girls; Philip had been right on that, but it seemed most of them with their consent. More general terms would be prostitution. He rested his elbows on his leather chair and his balding head shone in the lamplight overhead. An expensive suit now fit where possible after his gluttonous eating had his body bulging from places that didn't have fat before.

"Vega's son? What does he want with me? Only thing I need right now is to find my daughter!"

"He is the new Don with his father's territories. He has full control of everything. There is no one to contest him. He has come to find out where his father's wife is. I heard rumors, Don Santori, that he is in love with the girl. Now the way is clear for him and he has come to claim her since his father died." The soldier of fortune stopped speaking, and waited to state the most important topic of the visit. "He has news of your daughter."

"Really… then maybe we should show him in," and Santori sat up in the chair and prepared to meet the new Don.

Patrick Vega entered flanked by Mac and Alex. Patrick, dressed from head to toe in black, looked remarkably like his father looked twenty years ago. It gave Santori a shock. No doubt whose son he was.

"Sir, it is with great pleasure that I meet you. I believe you would also be Don Andrea as was your father," and Santori stood and stretched his hand to Patrick.

It hit Patrick hard. He was the new Don and his first task was one he would rather not have had. "Don Santori, my pleasure." Patrick glanced around the room. It was richly furnished, with reds and blacks and oil paintings hung from the walls. Even in this weather the fireplace was alive with burning and crackling logs.

"A seat, Sir, if you would."

Patrick sat on a chair of equal height to Santori. The whole room was full of bodyguards sporting rather up-to-date weapons.

"My consigliore says you have news for me. My daughter, I think. Is this true?" and he clicked his fingers, requesting a cigar and one for the new Don.

Patrick declined the offer. Mac and Alex had positioned themselves behind Patrick, both showing their possession of guns which had not been removed from them in the hallway by mutual consent.

"It is true, Sir. My associates have her. She is perfectly safe and being cared for," 'by my father,' he thought, "for now. We will be glad to hand her back to you for some very simple information."

"And that would be," Santori pretended not to know, a vacant look on his face.

Patrick stood up and flexed his new-found power. "I want Emma." That part was true. "I want to marry her." Again true. "But your associate, Marc, has her and we don't *yet* know where he is!"

"That's it, that's what you want? Then I get my daughter back? This young lady must be some kind of woman to capture two or three men's hearts. Indeed if I knew of her, I might want to keep her for myself. Marc has good taste."

"How do you know she is young?" Patrick asked quite casually. "Unless you have met her? I assume then you have. She has been here with Marc."

"Very astute. She was here but Marc took her away when he heard of your father's death, of which I was very sorry to hear about. A heart attack I heard."

"That is correct. The funeral is next week." Now he was adlibbing. This was not part of the plan. "So, Don Santori, do I get the information or not, and do you get your daughter back in one piece?"

Santori leaned back in the chair and puffed hard on the cigar that had just been lit by his consigliore.

"How do I know you have her? You could be making this up? And better still how did you get to her? Only one or two men could ever get in and out of here without being seen."

"Then I guess it was one of the one or two men that took her, wouldn't you think?" Patrick held his ground. His father would be proud of him. Alex and Mac certainly were. "If you need proof," and he turned to Mac for the proof.

Mac produced the bracelet that Janine had given them and handed it to Santori. There was something familiar about Mac, but Santori couldn't place him.

"That should prove to you that we have her. She is well hidden, somewhere close but a place you would not think to find her." Patrick was beginning to like this. "Like my father, I get what I want!"

Santori knew of Vega's prowess both in business and with women… especially his daughter and he had a feeling that his daughter probably went of her own free will because of her feelings for the late father.

"I can give any woman you want from here. One maybe two. You can choose." And a couple of the women stepped out of the shadows ready to do their master's bidding. "I cannot, though, tell you where Marc is, mainly because I don't know. He left in a great hurry with the girl as if the devil was after him even though he knew your father was dead. He was muttering something about a girl and a baby. Some girl back at your house was giving his friend, and my nephew, information and then it stopped very abruptly. So Marc never found out anything else."

Jillie. Had to be. At least he didn't bring up Donna and the baby. And he hadn't put two and two together about Vinnie. Guess they didn't know he was dead. Correction… that Philip Vega had killed him.

"Well, do we have a deal or not then? I do believe, Don Santori, that you know where Marc is. He would tell you. Even if he didn't, you have a number to reach him, correct?"

"Correct." Santori smiled. Like father like son. He didn't want to start off badly with this new Don. They had all been good friends once, both families. That was until Janine's baby, hers and Philip Vega's!

Chapter 33

They left the same way they came, but with a good phone number and a deal that Janine would be returned... unharmed. By evening they were back at Caroni's house for dinner; everyone including Janine Santori, who Don Caroni welcomed with open arms, treating her like his own daughter.

Janine was reminded to treat Philip like one of the hired guns. She was introduced to Patrick, who once more admired his father's taste in women, half wishing that she had been his mother.

Dinner was pleasant and one that Janine did not want to end. She knew that she would soon be home, back to her now boring life, or so she thought. She could see Andrea at the other end of the table. Once or twice she caught him staring at her and she thought of times long ago. She wondered if he had ever thought about the past.

Patrick had a call to make... to Marc or at least to one of his henchman. He wanted to hear Emma's voice. He wanted to see her, make sure she was safe--not just for his father, but for himself. He drank wine, a lot of wine. His father did also as did Mac. Charlie didn't touch a drop; neither did Alex, as they had been assigned to be the designated drivers.

"Don Caroni, I would like to thank you for the hospitality and for letting Janine Santori stay here today. Tomorrow she will be home at her father's and we will bother him no more unless the phone number turns out to be not so good. I will call him in a few moments and we will find out! Please excuse me," and Patrick stood as did Andrea and Mac, following Patrick out of the room.

"Ms. Santori, we have a room ready for you, should they wish you to stay the night here while they find Marc," and Caroni smiled at her, his older, wiser face seemingly understanding; his eyes wise from years of being a Miami Don.

"I would like that very much, Sir. Might I ask if I could borrow some night attire from someone in your household?" Janine still had on the same cocktail dress with one of Andrea's shirts on top.

"I am sure we can arrange that for such a lovely guest. And you will find everything you need already in your room. I bid you good-night all. I have some family matters to attend to," and Caroni stood as his consigliore helped him from his chair.

"Alex and I will show you to your room. Should you wish to visit with Andrea later to discuss events, I will be glad to swap rooms with you for, say, an hour," Charlie smiled a knowing smile at her.

She nodded and accompanied them up the stairs to her room. They left her at the door.

"In one hour, knock on the blue door next to Patrick's. You will find Andrea there." Charlie relayed his instructions from Philip, and they disappeared into Patrick's room.

Patrick was about to dial Marc's number, or what they thought was his number.

He had his instructions from his father. Philip, Mac and now Alex and Charlie waited with baited breath. Patrick had the phone on speaker.

"This is Patrick Vega. I would like to speak to Marc. Is this Marc's phone?"

There was a pause… a long one. "This is Marc," and the voice seemed deeper or distorted or something. "I was wondering when you would call. Santori give you this number? You must have some kind of hold on him. Following in your father's footsteps, Patrick?"

"Someone has to, Marc. A real son always does that," and Patrick realized that wasn't a smart move, especially when he looked at his father's face. "I've come to get Emma."

"You did, didn't you? But you can't have her, Patrick. I have her. I have money and I am building an empire down here for me…Marc whatever-my-last-name-is. What kind of hold do you have on Santori?"

Andrea nodded to tell him.

"We have Janine Santori and her father won't be very happy with you if he doesn't get her back in one piece. So I suggest that you let me meet with you and at least see Emma. Plus my father left you a considerable amount of money in his will."

This time there was a longer pause, so much so that Patrick thought the line had been disconnected and shook the phone.

"Okay. Tomorrow morning. Six a.m. The bridge on First Street by our old house. Be there…just you and one more. If I see anyone else, I don't show; neither does the love of your life." Then nothing.

Patrick was long passed being embarrassed by that remark.

"You all heard. Who goes?"

Vega didn't hesitate. "Mac. We will stay in the car at the end of the bridge. He doesn't know Charlie or me and would be suspect. Alex, Charlie and I will be by the SUV." Philip turned away from them then. Emma was alive; that's what counted.

He walked to the window, looked out at the city. Tomorrow he would see his wife again but she wouldn't see him. He turned to face his son. "You get her out of this, Patrick; what ever it takes."

"I'll get her, Sir…"

"Patrick, if you have to barter, give him as much money as he wants. Do not give him Donna and the baby, at any cost. No matter what. If all else fails… tell him, he can have me. Tell him… tell him I am not dead and I will give myself up to him and you will take Emma and leave here with her."

There was dead silence in the room.

Mac was the first one to speak. "You can't do that, Don Andrea. You just can't. Nothing is worth your life. You have a dynasty, territories and you have us." Mac was so serious and his blue eyes never faltered in their commitment.

Philip could not speak. Loyalty had come from the strangest source.

"She has to be safe, and I…well I have to dispose of your son, Mac. He cannot live!"

"I know that, Don Andrea. I know it well. And he shall not. But not by your hand. It is my duty… You have to take her home. You have your daughter there…"

Vega's eyes squinted. And he moved his head just slightly side to side. Had Mac figured all the things out?

"Change of plan. Patrick goes and I go as backup. End of story."

"You can't do that, Andrea…" Charlie stepped in.

"I can do what the fuck I like and not you or God can stop me!"

It was then they realized that Philip Vega didn't care anymore what happened to him. The drugs had worn off and he was in pain and fighting with himself to stay alive. Someone had to talk him out of it, and it was probably not a man that could do it; but maybe a woman could. Maybe Janine could talk him out of it…or at least make him stay.

Chapter 34

An hour later, Janine came to Andrea's room. Charlie had told her what happened and now it was her job to try to talk Andrea out of his suicidal scheme by any means possible, even to the point of seducing him and keeping him in the room.

Patrick's room was next door. He could hear them arguing. Not the best sign he had heard.

"Damn. I was hoping Janine could keep him here in the morning, but it doesn't even sound like she can keep control of him tonight," Charlie looked at Patrick. "Sorry, Patrick, that was clumsy of me."

"It's okay, Charlie. I am beginning to understand my father a lot more than I thought I could. I wish I was as adept at getting women as he obviously was and is! But he shouldn't be up there with me tomorrow. He most likely will pull his gun out and just shoot Marc. I don't think that shit is just going to hand her over to us. See her maybe, but not take her."

"You always loved her?"

"Right from the day my father brought her home. I can see why he fell for her. Long golden hair, bright green eyes, a body to die for. She weighs next to nothing and when she talks about my father she blossoms, like she has found God. He is everything to her. When he first introduced her, we thought how young she was; our age, you know, but she fit right in with us, took over with the twins like she was born to it. Even got along with Donna. And my father told you the truth. There have been no other women since her..." and he paused, thinking of Donna. "That we know of, that is. I just don't think he would do that to her, do you?"

"Truth…no. There has to be another explanation. Not sure what, but another. Maybe we should go and separate them before the whole house hears them."

"Maybe we should," and they both left the room and went next door and knocked quite loudly on the door.

Vega opened it. "And what the hell do you two want? Like I don't know! Don't ever try to 'fix' me up again! I don't do well with that," and he stormed past them both and into Patrick's room. "Patrick, a word!" and he went straight into the bedroom.

Charlie slipped into his and Andrea's room. Janine was almost in tears.

"I'm sorry, Charlie. I couldn't hold him. I tried. He was onto me like a shot; says he knew what you guys were doing. I failed you but most of all I failed him. I have never seen a man love a woman so much. He is obsessed with her; something I never thought I would see," and tears rolled down her face. "She has a hold that no woman ever has had on him," and Janine rushed into the bathroom.

Perhaps now was not the time for Charlie to share his theory with her, but he did have enough to do a DNA for her when they got home. "Janine," he tapped on the bathroom door, "we had to try. I'm sorry, really I am. I'll leave my number on the table here. Take it with you and stay in touch with me. I'll find out what I can about your daughter. You have my word on it." He paused, wishing they hadn't tried this. "Janine, again I am sorry. Patrick and I thought if anyone could keep him here…" Now he felt stupid. "I'm sorry…" and he left the room and went back to his own, leaving the way for her to excuse herself back into her own room. He had the feeling he wouldn't be very welcome in Patrick's room right now. On that he was right.

"What the fuck were you two doing? All you did was succeed in upsetting someone I once cared about very much." Philip was red in the face and so angry that Patrick didn't want to get any closer than he had to.

"Once? Sure it's not still?" Bad mistake and Patrick knew it.

"Patrick, enough! I won't take this shit even from you. You are my son and you will do as I say. Now get some sleep. Tomorrow you go for Emma, and you bring her back home to me, boy, you understand me? Do I make myself clear?"

Patrick all but withered under the icy stare. For once in his life he was frightened by the force of violence that his father exhibited.

"Yes, Sir…"

"Good. Now I am going back to my own room to get some sleep, and I hope it's empty except for Mac," Philip turned on his heel and left Patrick standing there.

Patrick raised his eyebrows, remembering he was the one who suggested that Janine meet him there. Patrick texted Mac to be very careful round his father, especially while he was carrying, and also sharing a room with him. There was a tentative knock on his door and Alex and Charlie stepped inside.

"Is it safe to come in? We could hear your father down the hall. I hope Don Caroni didn't hear him. Give all the game away." Charlie peeked round the door frame.

"I hope he didn't either. I have never seen him that angry before. Charlie, you said you thought Mr. Vega had taken something other than pain pills," Alex ventured into the conversation.

"Dad? He despises drugs. He would never do that!" retorted Patrick, confident his father would never do hard drugs.

"He would if the pain was bad enough and he had to get through this," Alex wasn't so sure.

"You think that's what he did?" asked Patrick as he walked to the door, listening there to make sure no one else could hear.

"Maybe. Mr. Vega is doing a lot of strange things right now. Is Mac with him?" asked Charlie, pulling on his beard.

"Yes. I told him to be careful. Mac isn't his favorite person right now. And I didn't help matters. Almost accused Dad of something going with Janine."

"I don't think it's Janine you have to worry about, Patrick. Donna maybe, but not Janine."

"You still on that, Charlie? I noticed you took an interest in the lady. After dad's old girlfriends now are we?" Patrick said with a hint of humor. "I heard you shared a lot when you two were younger. So did Pauli and my father, and apparently they still are. It's Pauli he asked to look after Donna." His own statement made him think.

"Patrick, you sound more like your father every day. And no, not in that sense. I just feel sorry for her. She was so glad to see him, helped us out, and he flung her aside." He paused. He couldn't tell them what he suspected. "I do think we should all get some sleep. Six a.m. is going to come round very fast and I don't think your father will tolerate your blowing this one, Patrick." Charlie moved to the door. "Come on Alex, let's go plot tomorrow and what we will do while your boss backs up his son. Mac will stay with Mr. Vega. We should check on Janine on the way. Last time I saw her she was crying her eyes out. I guess she wouldn't be the first woman to do that over Philip Vega, and I have a very strong feeling not the last!"

Chapter 35

Five o'clock came early. The conversation in Vega's room was at point zero. Meanwhile Charlie and Alex had a backup plan and had not had a chance to tell Mac except by a short text. Breakfast was a grab bag of croissants and juice as they passed by the kitchen. Philip was at the car first. The SUV's engine was already running and Caroni's man sat ready to go by five-thirty. Next came Patrick with Mac. They both looked at Vega, who stood next to the car smoking a cigarette. Hair pulled tightly back, moustache trimmed and now sporting stubble, clothes black from head to toe, and a gun sticking out of the front of his jeans and one in a shoulder holster. Patrick didn't even know his father had one. Had to be borrowed.

"Good morning." Patrick said in lowered voice. He seemed a little nervous as the mantle of the Vega dynasty rested on his shoulders… and so did Emma's life.

"Morning. We all ready to go?" Philip was looking for the rest of the group.

Then he saw Janine in the doorway of the house. She was dressed in someone's over large pajamas, hair askew, with a worried look on her face. Philip wanted to tell her he was sorry about last night. Tell her it was okay and they would be back and she would be free. But he couldn't do it, especially not in front of these men. That would be weakness and that wasn't on the menu. She only had to stay today. He could hear them talking right by him.

"Andrea…" Mac commented.

"Ready?" asked Patrick dressed very similar to his father and today did indeed look more like the old Philip than ever.

"Never more so!" replied Vega and dropped the cigarette to the floor, stamping it out like a life.

They piled into the car, Andrea in the front next to the driver. He checked his watch. Five-forty-five. Fifteen minutes before he would see Emma again. Nothing his men had done or said would stop him going this morning. Not even the pain in his chest. He had wanted to call Donna before they left, but it was way too early. She would be fine with Pauli. He would take care of them if anything happened here that didn't turn out so well. He had left papers in the safe just in case, declaring who got what and what would happen with the children if anything happened to him or Emma. Everything was taken care of. Patrick was the legal heir and guardian of all the children, everyone. And there was an abundance of money, mostly in cash. Pauli knew where.

His thoughts came back to the situation in hand. They were almost to the bridge. He knew this place well. It's where he used to live in a different life. One with his first wife and their children. No, not all his children. Marc was Mac's son. His own son was about to prove he was a man.

The sun rose in the sky, casting shadows in the early morning light. Street lights dimmed and disappeared as their car slowed down to face the on coming limo. The driver turned the headlights off and on again twice. This was the meet, the place to find out the truth. Was she alive? Would she be standing there? How would she look? Would she know him? Detect it was her lover? So many questions.

And then they were there, cars face to face. Marc stepped out of the car and his new- found wealth in the trafficking business, that and drugs. He was surrounded by a couple of bodyguards, all armed and all potentially dangerous.

Andrea was out of their SUV first and opened the door for his son. No words were needed between them, just a nod. Patrick stepped forward, the new Don. He kept on walking, Andrea six steps behind him, the rest of them back by the SUV.

Marc seemed like a different man. Arrogant and self assured, the way Vega was. If it hadn't been for the blonde hair and blue eyes, Vega would have thought he was his real son. Marc looked like his mother today, smoldering confidence surrounding him. He was dressed in expensive clothes, not ones he usually wore. He took a few steps forward, followed closely by two very heavily armed men. He smiled a crooked smile at Patrick.

"*Don Andrea*, how nice of you to come! Or may I call you Patrick?" and the sarcasm was there in full force.

"Patrick is just fine," and Patrick looked towards the limo. "I have come for Emma. We have Janine and she will be terminated unless Emma is returned to me. Don Santori will then find you and kill you, and everyone with you. You must give her back!"

"Must I? Why? She doesn't love you; neither does she love me, but I have her and you don't. I was sorry to hear that your father had died," and Marc laughed an evil laugh. "But at least you know who your father was. I don't even know that. You all know. The world knows, everyone knows, except me. Emma knows but she wouldn't tell me. Oh, I tried to make her tell me. I think I know, and then it slips away. But you know what? I don't really care anymore." He glanced behind Patrick. "New man I see, new bodyguard. Not happy with the old guard? Don't blame you. Only one I liked was Rossi. And Mac, he was the worst."

How Patrick wanted to tell him that was his father. End it right there.

When Marc looked at Vega it was as though he knew him. Resounding bells went off in his head. The man was a killer if ever he saw one. Patrick had come prepared to dance or die. He looked again. He knew him yet he didn't. This man had death surrounding him.

Patrick saw him watching his father. "Marc. I would like to see Emma. That was the deal. We get to see her to know she is alive, and then maybe Janine goes home."

Marc hesitated. "Bring her out!" and he yelled back to the limo.

The door swung open, and long black-stocking legs stepped out complete with very high black heels. A flash of short red silk dress came next, covering a slim and sexy body. Then came the shock. Her face was painted with bright red lipstick and strong black eyeliner.

But it was her hair that struck the most vital chord in them all. Gone were the long curly blonde locks. In place was short spiky dark brown hair. The bodyguard helped her stand. On her face was a vacant look. Gone was the gentleness of the Emma they knew. Here stood someone who had no clue as to who or where she was.

"Emma, walk to me," commanded Marc, and Emma did as he asked. "You see she is alive. Kind of. Been like that since we told her her husband was dead. That and drugs!"

"What the fuck did you do, Marc? What did you do to her?" and Patrick was almost yelling, so much so that everyone by the SUV could hear.

Emma stood still, her vacant eyes managed to focus on Patrick, and through the blur she knew him.

"Patrick?" Her voice was shaky. "Is he dead? Is Philip dead?"

"Yeah, Emma. It's me. Come to take you home. Your daughter needs you." Patrick was having a hard time trying to control his temper. He did not dare turn to look at his father for he had a feeling he could shoot Marc on the spot, the anger in him blowing his cover. "He is, Emma. He is dead." Betrayal did not come easy.

Philip Vega's eyes scanned her body. He couldn't tell if she was still pregnant or not. She was thin from drugs and lack of food but there didn't seem to be a baby bump on her. He wanted to run forward and grab her and shoot the bastard Marc right there and then, but that would not get her out.

"I will buy her from you. You always need money. Two million dollars in exchange for Emma, and we take her now." Patrick was trying to remain calm.

"I can make more than that in a month. How about ten million? Your father has it. I'm sorry; your dead father had it." Marc laughed and he grabbed at Emma, twisting her arm behind her back.

It was clear then that they would never see her alive again, if they didn't get her now.

It was then that Emma cried out in pain, and she looked up for help. Her eyes caught the blonde bodyguard watching her and the connection was there just as it always had been. Her eyes widened and she stopped squirming in Marc's grasp and stared at the blonde

Hells Angel. Philip tried hard to look away from her and could not take his eyes off her. She blinked her eyes, disbelieving.

Patrick saw the look on her face. "Ten million. You have my word. Now give her to me!" His voice was loud.

"A Vega's word is no good. Come back tomorrow..." and Marc looked at the bodyguard again and he turned to look at Emma, her eyes transfixed on him. Her mouth betrayed her and her husband with just one word as she breathed his name.

"Philip..."

And hell opened its doors and let the devil in.

Chapter 36

Philip knew she had made him and by the look on Marc's face he had, too. Vega's hand went to the gun in his jeans. He pulled it, and Patrick went for the one in the back of his. Emma saw it all in slow motion. She had hardly finished mouthing his name and now saw her husband very much alive. She squirmed in Marc's grasp trying to get to the safety of the road. Philip had always told her to lie flat if guns were drawn.

"Patrick, get out of the way. Drop down!" yelled his father and he aimed his gun straight at Marc, his .357 glinting in the dawn light; his stance that of a man ready to kill. He could see the two bodyguards next to Marc; one was ready to fire. It was now or never. Which one to go for? He thought Marc. That had been Mac's job and now it was his. But at least Emma would be free from his grasp.

Philip bent his knees just slightly and took aim at Marc, just as the bodyguard on the right took aim. Before the bodyguard had time to centralize his shot, Alex was there by Vega's side and a shot rang out from Charlie Hill's long distance rifle, the one with the telescopic lens. Bodyguard number two went down. Number one dropped to the ground with Alex's bullet deep in his chest, dead on impact. Only Marc remained standing.

"Let her go, and I will spare your life!" Vega didn't so much yell as growled in fierce anger. "Didn't you hear me? I will fire and drop you dead on the spot. Let her go!" Philip Vega was oblivious to the rest of the world. All he saw was Marc holding Emma back from getting to him. He leaned down just a little more, his aim at Marc's chest, deadly and accurate, waiting to kill him.

"Marc, do as Don Andrea says. Let her go! He will shoot you and with my blessing!" Mac came slowly up to Vega, his gait very deliberate, gun in hand. "Let her go. If he doesn't kill you, I will." He paused and with determination conceded at last. "And, Marc, I am your father."

The look on Marc's face was one of total shock. "I don't believe you!" he screamed. You cannot be. You are just a servant, a nobody. Vega's errand boy. His killing machine. No, that's not right, is it? He's the killer. Look at him, ready to kill me! And he could do it, too. You couldn't, not even to save Emma," and with that he pulled her by the arm until her body was almost his shield.

She struggled, but he was stronger. She looked toward Philip, her eyes pleading to him. Philip blinked his eyes. He'd been here before. Marc taking Emma from him and Mac… and now it came flooding back. Mac and Alex had been there that night at the Biltmore. Marc had won that night and he wasn't about to win again. Philip now had a second chance.

"Mac, if your son doesn't let her go right now, I will shoot him dead in cold blood. On that you have my word. Tell him!" and Don Andrea meant every word he said. "I will give him sixty seconds, starting now."

And Mac knew what he had to do. He had failed his Don once. He could not do it again. He raised his gun, his .22 and aimed at Marc's head.

"Don Andrea said let her go." As he spoke there was movement from the limo and the driver stepped out firing at the closet target, that being Mac. The first bullet hit Mac in his right shoulder and he turned sharply and fell, growling in pain, his gun dropping to the ground with a clanking noise. Charlie fired back, hitting his target instantly. His gun had never failed him.

It was then that Marc pulled his gun from the back of his jeans and slowly brought it round towards Emma's head, and it was then that Philip Vega fired and as by the true rules to die by, hit him square between the eyes.

Marc went down to the ground, blood spurting from his face, and Emma dropped with him. One clean shot was all it took to end his life.

Vega's stance was the same as if frozen in time. Alex stepped beside him and lowered the smoking gun in Don Andrea's hands. Charlie rushed forward to Emma and pried Marc's hand from Emma's arm. He helped her stand, the rifle in his other hand. Then he could see clearly the bruises on her arms from fingers holding her way too tightly. Vega must not see these right now and he slipped his old jacket off and, laying his rifle on the ground, slid the jacket around her shoulders. He watched her face, her eyes staring in disbelief.

"Emma, you're safe. It's Charlie Hill, your husband's friend. Let me take you to him," and he picked up the rifle and ushered the terrified young woman across the roadway.

In the background, sirens could now be heard. Police fast approaching. Time to leave this place.

"Mac," yelled Charlie, "can you stand? We need to leave! We cannot be caught here." Too many questions and no answers. "Patrick, help Mac. Get him into the car. Now!"

Philip Vega still stood, knowing what he had done. He had killed Marc, who was once a Vega. Then he saw Emma and even through her tears she could see his face.

"Philip," she cried. "Philip…" and she flung herself at him. "They told me you were dead."

Philip pushed his gun in his jeans and grabbed hold of his wife. He threw his arms round her and his hands clung to her back, Charlie's jacket almost in the way. She tried to hold him as tightly as she could and he winced in pain. Hiding it was something else.

"Boss, we have to go. They cannot find you here." And Alex tried to usher them both into the SUV.

Patrick slung his arms around Mac's shoulder and aided the blood-stained man into the car. It was then he noticed that there was blood everywhere. Why hadn't he seen that? Why hadn't he been part of it? Mainly because when the time came his father was the one who was the killer and exercised the rules. He was still the Don and had proved it tonight. All they left behind were dead men and bloody streets. And one of those was Mac's son still lying where he fell. No witnesses, none to tell the story.

Six of them piled into the car, Emma hardly knowing where she was. Only that she was safe and her husband was alive. Caroni's driver sped up the departure and the SUV left there in a great hurry, sirens getting louder in their ears.

Back streets came in handy and it was a narrow escape, with the morning rush hour through Miami doing little to help the escape. Sirens passed them, speeding cop cars, and in the SUV Mac moaned in agony, the bullet firmly lodged in his shoulder.

Emma looked up at her husband from where she lay on his lap curled up in a ball. She looked hard at him and for the first time since she had met him, she hardly knew him, not just because of the blue eyes and blonde hair, but because of the look on his face. And he looked down at her, wanting to make love to her right there and then, wanting to kiss her, tell it was all going to be okay and knowing maybe it wasn't. Not this time.

Chapter 37

Philip pulled Emma as close as he could to him. How he loved her and knew that when the truth came out he might lose her for good. He could still feel the pain in his chest and the one in his heart. He had killed Mac's son. Maybe better than father killing son. He touched Emma's hair and stroked it, and she cried into his chest, tears falling down his body like feathers in the rain.

Patrick sat next to him and he couldn't take his eyes off Emma or his father. They were like one, Ying and Yang. There was more than envy there.

Philip knew it.

Mac sat in the front and was slumped down in the seat. Blood dripped down his arm onto the black leather upholstery. Alex leaned over the seat and tried to stem the flow with anything that came to hand. Charlie leaned back on the seat and tried to comprehend what had happened back there. They were all dead, every one of the limo party...and Marc, Mac's son...gone just like that. He turned his head to look at Vega, whose face was almost buried in his wife's hair, and he swore he could see tears in his friend's eyes. He had to admit he would not have wanted the job of ending Marc.

They were now able to speed through the outskirts of town and back to Caroni's house. The driver called ahead and Don Caroni's personal doctor was on hand for both Emma and Mac. The SUV screeched into the driveway and stopped in front of the house.

Caroni's men were there in abundance and helped the wounded Mac into the house. Philip stepped out of the car and Patrick helped Emma into his father's arms. Vega scooped her up and carried her into the hallway of the house. She was tucked into him like a little child, her arms clinging round his neck. Alex wondered how Philip was managing to carry her with the pain he knew he still had in his chest. He offered to at least open doors for his boss.

As Vega carried his wife up the stairs to Patrick's much better furnished room, he saw Janine in the hallway watching. He felt bad for her but now was not her time. That was gone and long past. But he did have the manners to ask for help for her.

"Charlie, look after Janine for me. Don't let her go just yet, and check on Mac for me. Send Patrick up also. No one besides us knows who I am. To the driver, I was shooting as a bodyguard, unless he heard Mac, which I doubt. Could have been me or Patrick he was talking to, and that's the way it should stay till we are out of Florida," and he entered the bedroom with Emma still in his arms.

Alex left them, darting down the stairs as Patrick made his way up. Charlie turned to Janine and ushered her into the bedroom.

"That's Emma? She's his wife? She looks more like his daughter. She's so little and slim…and…" Janine couldn't find the words.

"And drop dead gorgeous. Yeah, we all know that. Patrick especially knows. And Andrea would give his life for her and almost just did. Right in the line of fire. You would have been proud of him, I know." And Charlie thought about it then, "We all were." Charlie meant it. He really did. They were proud of Andrea even though they hadn't told him. Charlie thought that maybe he should stay with Janine. Maybe Patrick was right. He did like Janine. He knew he felt sorry for her and he would do his utmost to help her find her daughter.

In Patrick's room, Philip still held Emma in his arms. Patrick came through the door with Alex.

"How's Mac?" asked Vega, genuinely concerned for his man.

"Doc's with him now. Don Caroni has them in a downstairs room. The driver heard nothing and said nothing. He just thought you were an extremely accurate bodyguard." Alex looked at Emma. "How is she?"

"Haven't had chance to find out yet," and Philip turned his attentions to his wife. "Emma," he whispered to her. "Baby…you can let go. Emma…" and he leaned into her face. "Honey…"

Emma looked up into his face. "They told me you were dead. I prayed you would come for me." She had no idea the others were even in the room. "I prayed, Philip, me," and she let out a laugh before she cried, bitterly; long, racking sobs that didn't stop.

Both men felt they were intruding, Patrick especially.

Philip sat down on the bed and gently rested Emma beside him. She let go just a little and Alex moved forward and pushed pillows behind her. She jumped just slightly.

"It's only Alex, Baby. Patrick's here, too. The doctor will be up soon. Here, let's get you out of that jacket. Patrick, help me with her," asked his father.

Patrick moved around the bed and leaned over to her. She was so thin and frail that he wondered if she would ever be the same woman again… The woman that his father wanted so badly. You could see it on his face.

Philip raised her up a little and Patrick slid the jacket off her. Her arms were black and blue and there were needle marks.

Patrick could hardly look his father in the face, and he knew it was a good thing that Marc was dead. He had done everything to Emma that Vega despised. And Philip was doing to himself what he despised more than anything.

Emma hardly noticed Patrick. All she wanted was Philip.

All thoughts were interrupted as there was a knock on the bedroom door. Alex opened the door and in came the Doc.

He was a typical mob Doc who knew his way around mob guys, but this patient was a female and one who was very obviously attached to the man in whose arms she lay. And a very tough man at that.

"Everyone out of the room, except this gentleman. You know her?" What mob Doc wanted, he got. Tall Italian with a gun in his little black bag of tricks.

"I know her…" Philip answered and he kept a tight hold of her hand.

Outside in the hallway Patrick and Alex stood. Charlie came out to see them.

"How is she? Any permanent damage?"

"Doc is with her, Charlie ... and the boss."

"Anyone know who 'he' is?" asked Alex.

"No. As soon as Emma and Mac can travel, we should leave Caroni and his family. Marc might be dead but Santori sure isn't. He will find out about Vinnie at some point and we don't want Janine brought into this," added Charlie.

They hadn't seen Janine follow Charlie out of the room. "I'm already in this though, aren't I? Andrea brought me into it, just like he always did," and the love she had had now brought resentment when she saw Emma in Philip's arms and the obvious love he had for his wife, a kind he never had for her.

Chapter 38

"**S**he was pregnant, Doc. Can you tell if she still is?" Philip pitched right in.

"Bit personal for a bodyguard, isn't it? Isn't this lady Don Andrea's wife?"

Philip raised his eyebrows. How did he know that? "It is. Question's the same, can you tell?"

"Yours?" Doc half turned to watch the reaction on the man's face.

"Mine!"

Now was the doc's turn to raise his eyebrows. "Can't tell. Better get her own doc to check that. I see by her arms she has had a couple of doses of drugs. More to control her I would think. Don't think that would do any lasting damage to her. Was she always this thin?"

"No. That's recent." Vega kept his words to a minimum.

"Give her lots of liquids and rest. I assume *you* are taking her back to Los Angeles?"

"I am."

"Then make sure she has everything she needs. Private jet?"

"As they come."

"Physically she will be fine; mentally depends if you can pull her out of it. She will need a lot of support from…" Doc stopped aware he was not quite sure who he was talking to.

"Me!"

"Right, 'you'! Nasty scar you have there. Looks recent. Go down a long way?"

"Stomach."

"Hurt much?"

"Like hell."

"Taking anything for it?"

"I was. I ran out. Pain killers."

"You want me to look at it while I am here?"

Vega nodded his head. "Baby, let go of my hand for a minute," and Philip pulled free from Emma's grasp and she lay back on the pillows, unaware of what was really going on.

Doc noted the 'Baby'.

"You trusted?" Vega asked.

"I'm trusted! Been with Caroni for a very long time. It's also doctor-patient confidentiality."

Philip raised his sweater. The scar was red and swollen.

"It's infected. Did you by any chance take the bandages off yourself?" Doc also noticed the black hair down to Vega's stomach.

"I did."

"You been taking anything else for it?"

"I did. I made a mistake."

"Darn right you did. Didn't Don Andrea dislike men who took drugs?"

Getting too close. Doc knew or at least thought he knew. Philip paused before he answered.

"He did, but he's not here to judge me, is he?"

"No, Sir. He is not." Doc fished in his little black bag. "Take these. Just painkillers, and take my advice and get your own personal doc to check you out also. Now I must go back to Mac. The bullet has to come out if you are to fly him home. He's tough. He'll be fine, and so will your…" Doc almost said it. "So will Mrs. Vega." Doc stopped. "Sir, does Don Caroni know you by any other name?"

"No and safer they do not know here!"

"Agreed. Good luck!" and Doc left the way he came.

Vega followed him and locked the door behind him. They needed space.

Philip sat down on the side of the bed. He stroked Emma's face, ran his hands through her short spiky hair and she responded to him. Her face turned to him and she whispered his name.

"You have blue eyes, Philip, and blonde hair. But I knew you. I would always know you. I heard some of what Doc said. Am I still pregnant? Am I still carrying your child? I tried to fight Marc. I tried so hard..." and she wept again, just gently so that tears ran down his fingers.

Philip leaned down and kissed them away and his mouth moved onto hers. He had to show her that it didn't matter what Marc had done. He slid his hand just slightly under the hem of her red silk dress, his fingers lingering on the top of the stocking. He hesitated just briefly, making her wonder if he thought she had been raped.

"He didn't..." and she couldn't say it.

"I know, Baby. You fought him," and he slid his hand up further, moving the dress with it. He glanced down. Black underwear greeted him, black silk. And he couldn't wait. He pulled them down from her body, his other hand searching for the hooks in her bra. She was breathing hard and so was he, both longing to be together again. In all his pain, he had to make love to her, right then and there. The black silk was gone and the dress was so easy to rip away from her. He could see her clearly now, her body thin and bruised, but still he pursued his wife. He all but lay on her, trying not to cause her any more pain, and he released his jeans himself.

Even though pain shot through his chest, he had to go on, had to prove to her and to himself that he wanted her back.

Emma reached up and pulled his head down onto her breast as she moaned quietly and again whispered his name as though she was calling for him.

He looked her in the face, his warm breath on her cheeks. "No matter what, Emma, I love you. I will always love you and you are the only woman I ever want. You are mine, Emma, and only mine," and Philip kissed her so passionately that she couldn't breathe.

She returned his kisses two-fold and reached down into the open jeans. Vega was ready and waiting for his wife and together they found each other. He was gentle with her at first and then love and lust became one, not once but twice. Her hands pulled on his hair and long strands of blonde fell from the band, and Philip subdued her cries with his mouth.

Coming together was something they had long ago achieved. He held her to him, rocking her gently to bring her down as quietly as he could.

And now she was his again, just like before. In Janine's room, where they all sat waiting for any news, both Patrick and Janine knew that both Emma and Philip were together again… as one.

Chapter 39

Philip gave her a few minutes. She needed time to recover from his ardent love making, which she probably wasn't up to right now; but she wanted him as much as he wanted her.

"Need the bathroom, Baby? Want to shower? I'll come with you," and then he realized she hadn't seen his chest in his haste to make love to her. If she saw the scar all the way down to his stomach…

He needed to shower, too…

"Baby, come on. Let me help you," and he picked her up in his arms and carried her into the bathroom. "I kinda like your hair like that, Emmy. Except it makes you look even younger. Folks will be thinking I am your father!" He laughed, just a little, and set her in the shower, pulled off his clothes and climbed in with her. If he kept sideways to her, maybe she wouldn't notice. He planned to occupy her in there anyway, and then he would climb out before her.

It worked. They showered together, made love again, slowly and lovingly, step by step until both of them were fulfilled. Water ran down them both, and rich soapy suds flowed over their bodies, hiding some of the scar. The soap stung him painfully, but he wanted to be with her, feeling his temper rise as he looked at her body covered in bruises. Marc was dead, but Mac wasn't. That wasn't a good thought. He kissed her gently, and then stepped out of the shower, wrapping a towel round his waist.

"Philip, don't leave me," she begged.

"I'm right here, Baby, and I'm never going to leave you again, not for any reason!" As he half-turned to talk with her, she saw the scar.

Her hand flew to her mouth. "My God, Philip. What happened to you? Did they do that to you? Did Marc and Vinnie do that? Did they?" she screamed at him over the running water.

Philip reached into the shower and turned off the tap, handing her a large fluffy towel. She wrapped it around her body and waited for her husband to reply.

"No, Baby. I did, when I thought I had lost you. I couldn't go on. So I shot myself and tried to end it all… you have my heart, Emma. I gave it you and I'll never take it back," and Philip Vega cried, slumping down to the floor, almost ashamed of himself.

Emma all but fell out of the shower. "Oh, my God, Philip. Oh, my God," and she dropped on the floor beside him and cradled him in her arms.

How long they stayed like that, neither of them knew. All she could think was that she had nearly lost him, and it was all because of her.

Maybe she should let someone know. But she was sure they would know. He was normally the strength, and now that task had fallen to her. She had watched him kill someone yet again today, this time someone he had loved, this time for her.

"Philip," she whispered. "Oh, Philip. I only went on because of you," and Emma cried also. "I have your heart, Philip and you have had mine from the day I saw you…"

He turned her in his arms, caressing her face between his hands and very sensuously he kissed her, feeling the reality of her words.

They were quiet then, each knowing everything there was to know. He a Godfather with a soul… and Emma knowing how much he really loved her.

He'd left his cell on the bed and now it rang continuously. It stopped and then rang again, disturbing their world.

"You have to get that?" she asked.

"Yeah, I should. Probably one of them is wondering where we are." Philip rose up and took her hand, leading back into the bedroom. He grabbed the cell without looking who it was. "Yeah?"

"Philip? You said to call you if I needed to. I just wanted to hear your voice. Make sure you are okay." A little voice asked.

Bad timing. "I'm fine. We have Emma back," and Philip realized that Donna didn't know that the possible father of her child was dead. "Baby, is Pauli near you? Can you put him on the phone?" There was a long pause. "Pauli, Philip. Yes, I have Emma. Pauli, I shot Marc dead. I don't know how to tell Donna. You will tell her? Thank you. We are leaving this afternoon for home. Mac has a bullet in him, but he can fly. Emma? She'll need rest, but she's fine. As soon as we land, it should be safe for you to go home. She okay there and the baby?" He remembered not to say Andrea. "I'll call you as soon as we land. Please be careful. We are not out of the woods yet!" And he disconnected the call.

Emma thought she heard him say "Baby", a name reserved for her, but maybe not. She also thought she heard Donna's name but she was tired and hungry. She needed food and she also needed some clothes. All she had was underwear, and there wasn't much of that.

Philip dropped the cell back onto the bed, and it rang again before he even had time to explain to Emma what was happening back in California. This time Philip looked at the name.

"Yeah, Patrick…she's fine. We both are. I need some clothes for her. Was going to borrow yours but I think they are too big. Can you go into my room and get mine? I need some also. Get my bag. I'll unlock this door and you can come in. Everyone else with you except Mac? How's the lady?" Philip listened. "Thought she might be. Did she find clothes? If she did, ask her to get some for Emma. Anything is fine; just so she is dressed. We should get some food in us all and get out of here. Caroni should not be involved anymore than he is. Come down to us." Philip disconnected the call. "Patrick's coming to the room, Baby."

"Patrick's here with us? I don't remember seeing him. I must have been right out of it." She had a blank look on her face. "I remember you shooting Marc," and she shivered, as she thought back, "and I remember Mac being shot. Where is Mac? Is he okay?"

"He's fine. Or he will be. Patrick's coming to bring you some clothes. You have underwear around here somewhere," and Philip started looking for it. He was still concerned for Emma. Everything was not coming back to her and he wondered what else she had forgotten…maybe something with Marc she was blotting out. "Emma, sit down for a second before Patrick gets here." She did and he continued. "There is a lady here who helped us to get to Marc, Janine Santori. I think you may have met her father, Don Santori. Well, she's here at this house, Don Caroni's estate, and today she will return home. I want you to meet her, Baby. Without her we would not have found you. There is so much to tell you, Emma." He paused long enough so that Emma could jump in.

"And she helped you because you knew her before?"

Philip was surprised. "Yes, she and I were what you would call young lovers. Lasted a very long time before I met Sally. She helped us find you though, Emma and that's what counts."

"Philip, I trust you. If she helped you then it's fine," and Emma smiled at him. She long ago learned to trust him, but she did have a feeling he was hiding more than he was saying.

Philip wondered how she would feel when she did know about Donna. He shuddered thinking about it. There was so much he had to tell her, and he hoped to God she understood.

As if on cue, someone knocked on the door. Philip grabbed his jeans and pulled them on, dropping the towel on the bed. He looked at Emma with the towel wrapped tightly round her. No one could see anything he didn't want them to see. The bruises he could not hide. He glanced at the bed. Disaster area and what had gone on very obvious to anyone.

He unlocked the door and was surprised to find both Patrick and Janine there. Philip had no choice but to let them both in, as Janine was carrying clothes for Emma.

Patrick looked at his bed, what was left of it, raised his eyebrows to his father and cut his eyes to Janine. Philip had not thought she would come with him.

There was no choice but to make introductions.

"Emma this is the lady I was telling you about, Janine Santori. She helped find you. Janine this is my wife, Emma… and the love of my life, and possibly the only woman I ever really loved." There, it was said.

Chapter 40

Electricity filled the room. Compared to Janine, Emma was a child. But nonetheless Andrea loved her enough to marry her. Janine was polite.

"Mrs. Vega. I am pleased to meet you. Your husband talks of nothing but you. In fact, even the other night he was telling me about you. Isn't that right, Andrea?" and she looked his way. "I'm sure he told you we were lovers years ago. Grew up together, in fact."

Emma wondered what she had done to this woman, having never seen her before.

"Ms. Santori. *Philip* has told me about *many* women before me and that's his business. I am sure you fit in there somewhere. If they are after me, *then* it's my business, but not before," and Emma smiled, as she ran her fingers through her waif-like hair. "You brought clothes for me. Thank you so much."

Emma saw the look that Patrick gave her husband. Maybe she hadn't imagined the word "Baby" after all, but now was not the time to bring it up. She took the clothes from Janine. "Do excuse me while I get dressed." She turned to her husband, who looked more than angry at Janine's display. "I'll be right back, Philip," and Emma leaned up to kiss him most purposefully on the mouth. He responded instantly, and, as she moved away from him, smacked her just lightly on her backside, a wry smile on his face.

He waited until she closed the bathroom door and then turned to look at Janine, his face still angry.

"What the fuck did you do that for? I just got my wife back and you spout that crap at her. She's already very upset from all this and now that? This is far from over and you and I know that!" He stopped, aware that Emma could probably still hear him. He brought his voice down lower. "What you and I had was then, not now," and he grabbed the clothes that Patrick had brought him and pulled the sweater over his head. "It's a scar, right? Just a damned scar, so stop staring at it like that, Janine," and Philip pulled his damp hair through the top of the sweater. He reached for his gun and pushed it down the back of his jeans. Philip sat down on the end of the bed and pulled his jet black boots on and proceeded to stuff the other gun inside one of them.

Patrick never took his eyes off his father. Even he realized that Janine had taken it too far. It wasn't called for. As far as Patrick was concerned, Janine was out of line and he didn't like her being rude to Emma. That was really uncalled for.

Philip calmed down, just a notch. "This has been a trying day for all of us. I think that you should return home. What you tell your father is your business. Just keep my real name out of it. Tell him you were kidnapped by Patrick here. Do not let him know I am alive, not right now anyway. Don't let anyone know right now, and keep Don Caroni way out of this. He doesn't even know I am here, let alone alive. Are we clear?" He stood up and maintained his full height again. "Janine, are we?" He looked into her face.

"Yes. I thought I could handle seeing you with your wife… and I couldn't. I should have stayed out of the room. Charlie will take me home. He already offered," and there was genuine sorrow on her face. "Tell her I am sorry."

The bathroom door opened. "Tell me yourself, Ms. Santori." Emma was dressed in boy's cuffed jeans and a shirt with the sleeves rolled up. She picked her high heels up from the place Philip had thrown them and slipped them on, giving her five feet another three inches. She leaned against Philip and he slid his arm round her, proud as ever of his wife.

"I'm sorry, Emma. Your husband is a very good and loyal man. I was sorry to lose him, but I'm glad he found you," and Janine smiled at her and then at Philip Andrea. She opened the door and left them.

"Wow, Dad. You really did have a complicated life."

"Yeah, I do…" Philip stopped. He didn't say "did". He said "do". Emma heard this time, loud and clear.

"Philip, would you take me to get some food? I'm very hungry."

"Baby, I'm sorry. What was I thinking?" and he realized she had noticed what he said. "Patrick will take you. I cannot. It will blow my cover here and Caroni is already far too involved. I'll be right down. I need to get Charlie to take Janine home and I should go see Mac. I cannot imagine how he feels right now. I should have gone down to see him before now."

"You should. I was taking up all the time… Mac is your friend; you go and see him. You can tell me later anything else you need to. And Philip, whatever you have to do to get us home safely, you do it. I love you, Philip," and she slipped her arm in Patrick's and they left the room.

Philip stared after her. She had heard him say "Baby", and, like Janine knew, he only reserved that pet name for women he slept with. Little did she know for whom else. If she had thought about it, she would have known. He also called their two-year-old daughter the same name.

He followed them down the stairs and then departed to where Mac was. He found him extensively bandaged, looking pale and drawn but alive, which was more than his son. Philip sat down next to him on the couch that was acting as a bed.

"How you feeling?" Philip knew that was a stupid question.

"Probably like you. How's Emma?" Mac was genuinely concerned.

"She's doing, okay. Not sure she remembers everything and maybe that's for the best." He paused, stood up and paced the room, shutting the double doors into the hallway. "Mac, Marc didn't leave me any choice. I had to save her…"

"I know, Sir. I know. If you hadn't, I would have. He left neither of us a choice." And Mac's voice was full of sorrow. "Did we leave him there on the road?"

"Yeah, Mac, we did. We did." Philip wasn't proud of that fact. "Doesn't seem like they traced us to here, but we need to leave Caroni's house, and," Philip paused, "we need to get Janine home. Charlie is going to take her, and then we'll all go to the airport. She didn't do well around Emma."

"What did you expect, Boss? Lovers don't play well together. Past or present."

"Mac, there is something I need to share with someone before I go crazy...it's about Donna...I..."

The doors opened and Charlie and Janine appeared.

"Going to take her home, Andrea. Think it would be better. All Caroni knows is that she helped Patrick lead us to Marc and Patrick's bodyguard killed him."

Philip stopped speaking to Mac. "Sounds good, Charlie." Philip looked at Janine. "Thank you for the help. I really do appreciate it."

"It was my pleasure. By the way, I left your shirt on the bed." Janine was almost in tears. She would never see him again. She moved forward to hug him and stopped. He wasn't hers to hug. He had a wife... a very young and pretty one, just what she would expect from Andrea Vega.

When they left, Emma and Patrick watched from the dining room doorway. Emma didn't want to talk to Janine again. They wandered toward the lounge to find Philip. Emma had eaten her fill, the first time in almost two weeks. She patted her stomach, and then she remembered.

Chapter 41

Four o'clock saw them all at the airport. Sad goodbyes had been said at Caroni's house. The Don was sad to see Vega's son go, and Philip had a hard time not to reveal who exactly he was. When Don Caroni said goodbye, he said it verbally to the other bodyguards. When it was Philip's turn, he shook his hand… and Philip almost told him. Caroni hugged Emma and Emma's eyes filled up as he whispered to her.

"Your husband was a great man, but I am sure that the one they call Andrea will take good care of you." He smiled at her in a fatherly way and then let her go.

And now it was time to board the jet. All of them. Janine was back home, and Charlie and she had promised to stay in touch. He actually liked her and he had the feeling that one day she might like him enough to visit him or vice versa.

The takeoff was bad. The plane lurched into headwinds that came from nowhere. And the plane rocked from side to side. Emma was promptly sick, missing her clean clothes by inches. Turbulence or still pregnant? Too soon to tell.

Philip was concerned for her and he ushered her to the back of the plane where they sat apart from the others. She leaned on him and Charlie thought Janine was right. She did look a lot more like his daughter than his wife. Twenty years difference was a lot.

He filled her in about Jillie and Vinnie. Most of the details, not all, especially not telling her how he himself had killed him. She didn't need to know that. Jillie was harder to explain. He told her about the affair with Jillie's mother. Philip didn't make excuses; just told her plain fact. He told her everything except the one thing she wanted to know, and that was about Donna. He told her where Donna was and that she was with Pauli, but not why, except that she had given birth and she was in danger until both Marc and Vinnie were dead. But they *were* dead, so why weren't they just going home?

They ate; Philip drank scotch and downed a couple of pain pills. He shared some with Mac, who seemed to be in better spirits now he was away from Florida. They all slept a little, Emma across her husband's lap. Alex sat with Mac on Vega's instructions, making sure he had everything he needed. Patrick and Charlie discussed everything they could about the situation.

"You going to help Janine find out where her daughter is? And better still, *who* she is?"

"I am going to try. I think…that if your father opened up, we might know more." Charlie went to light up a cigarette and thought better of it. He chewed on gum instead. Smoking next to a man with a gunshot wound wasn't smart.

"You think Jillie is Janine's daughter? Really?" asked Patrick, his eyes popping.

"Maybe. Maybe not. Someone somewhere knows the truth. Your father may not know. The baby may have been adopted and Jillie's mother may have made up the story to Andrea, leading him to think there was another child that died at birth. He does admit to the affair with her, though, but once again the timing is off. Your father got around, Patrick. Glad to see you are not following in his footsteps," and Charlie laughed, realizing his own joke. "Well, I guess you have, haven't you…loving Emma the way you do."

"I've been thinking about that. I should move out of the house. Get my own place for a while and give them space. If Emma is still pregnant they need to be alone more." Patrick was growing up slowly and it showed lately.

"Patrick, Andrea can never be alone again. When Santori finds out your father killed Vinnie, someone will pay. Both you and the bodyguards will be on twenty-four-seven until it's ended. Always remember that. And always remember you can call on me! I still want my Ferrari." Hill had a wistful look on his face.

"I think you will get your car, Charlie. My father doesn't break his word!" and Patrick gazed down the plane at him. He wondered if that statement was true.

"Good. I need a new car. Then Andrea and I can race along Pacific Coast Highway..." and Charlie laughed and smacked his leg with his hand. "Course, your father will win. He drives like he lives... fast!"

"That he does, Charlie. That he does." He paused. "Charlie, what do you think is going on with Donna?"

Charlie changed instantly. "I truthfully don't know. I wish I did. I think that Mac intends to find out though. Marc was his son and the baby could be his grandchild. If he is and they prove that, he will want part custody of baby Andrea with Donna, unless..."

"Unless what, my father is the father and not Marc or Vinnie?" Patrick was almost afraid of the answer.

"Something like that, yeah. He is being very secretive about her. I doubt he told Emma. She's too calm... and more than likely still pregnant with his child."

"My God, that would be a mess. They would fight for partial custody... and Donna...what would she do?" asked Patrick.

"Who knows? And Andrea, with his power, would win if he's the father and lose Emma for good!"

Patrick hadn't thought of that angle. Emma would leave his father. Surely to God there was another explanation. There had to be.

"He wouldn't risk it, not even Dad would be that stupid, to risk a one night stand with Donna and lose Emma. He loves her, Charlie. You can see the way he looks at her. For goodness sake, he shot himself over her."

"Did he? Or did he shoot himself because of the mess he had made of his life with various women?" Charlie had said that out loud and he wished his brain thought more before it conveyed stupid messages to his mouth.

"You don't think that, do you?" Patrick spun around in the seat from watching his father and looked at Charlie Hill.

"No! I don't! I don't even know why I said it." Charlie watched Andrea and Emma just like Patrick had done. Andrea did indeed love this girl; now all he had to do was prove it to all of them, but most of all to her.

The plane landed on time, a good landing at Santa Monica airport on the private runway. They had the Ferrari and the SUV still parked there. Anthony had sent another car just in case and the good news that all the family was fine. And that Jillie was still under lock and key. Only one piece of news was disturbing. Rossi had taken a drive and not returned. Philip's party took the cars and drove back to Charlie's place.

At Hill's place Vega called Pauli. There was no answer. He tried again. Still nothing. He tried Donna's cell. Again nothing.

He told Charlie and Patrick. And then Emma.

"Baby, I have a quick stop to make. You go home with Patrick and Mac. Philipa is anxious to see her mommy, and so are the boys. I have to find out why Pauli is not answering his phone. He took Donna to my father's old hunting lodge like I told you on the plane. She was to be safe there until we got back. They were not to leave there until I called Pauli. Baby, I have to go find them…"

"I understand that Philip. I will be fine until you get back. I will be surrounded by your men… go, Philip. Go find them," and she reached up and kissed him in front of them all, something she very rarely did.

Philip grabbed hold of her and kissed her back passionately in front of his own crew. Charlie watched his friend.

"Has to be another reason… has to be, Patrick. Just like I said."

Chapter 42

"Patrick, please take Mac and Emma and go home. Anthony has sent you extra bodyguards and you will be fine. Alex and Charlie, with me." He let go of Emma, almost reluctantly.

"Where are you going, Philip?" She asked her eyes wide and really wanting to know.

"I have to go find them. Rossi took a drive!" Philip stated.

That's all they needed to hear to spring into action.

"Baby, go with Patrick. You guys take the SUV. Charlie, you and Alex take the Ferrari. It's faster."

"And how will you get there, Andrea? Like I couldn't guess?"

"Your Harley!"

"How did I know that would be the answer? Do I get to keep your Ferrari?"

"No! Mine has my tags. Yours won't! Now, let's just do this!" Philip tried the number again. Still nothing. Something was seriously wrong. One cell out, maybe. Two, no coincidence.

"Patrick, get her home and look after her. Do not let anyone go near Jillie till I get back. Understand?" Vega was back in full command.

"Yes, Sir…" and Patrick escorted Emma into the SUV along with Mac and some serious looking henchman from the estate.

Seated in the car, Emma looked back at Philip as he disappeared with Charlie around the back of the house. Suddenly she could hear the loud gunning of a motorcycle. Her heart missed a beat as around the corner her husband appeared astride the Harley. She watched him as he showed no fear and looked like he was born to it. No helmet and his hair loose from its mooring on the back of his head.

Mac was watching too. "Never changes, Emma. He will always be the hotshot he is."

Emma thought that a strange statement in light of the circumstances. All she could see was the Hells Angel she'd slept with.

The next noise they heard was the Ferrari with Charlie at the wheel, living his dream. One day this would be his, or close enough. Alex sat beside him, already looking uncomfortable as he waited for the ride to begin. Philip banged his fist on top of the car and then was gone up the drive of Charlie Hill's place, doing ninety on the Harley with his Ferrari right behind.

Emma stared after them, knowing that this had to be important to leave her behind.

"Emma, he'll be fine. He's been riding since he was a teenager. You didn't know, did you?"

"He never told me," she murmured, her face unreadable.

"Seems there is a lot he forgot to mention to you!" Patrick whispered so she couldn't quite hear, and he turned away to look after Mac.

"She okay?" Mac asked Patrick.

"I hope so. Why did he go with Charlie? Couldn't he have sent them on their own?"

"This time, no. He was right to go. Only Pauli and I know where the lodge is. I couldn't go and the rest speaks for itself. It's hard on Emma though. She really needs him and to be honest, I don't know what kind of condition he is going to be in when he comes back!"

"What's that supposed to mean?" Patrick's face very serious. "You know more than you are letting on, don't you? Something to do with Donna?"

"Keep your voice down, Patrick. I don't know anything. But your father was about to confide something in me when Charlie and Janine came into the room. He mentioned Donna's name. He's got to see this through however it plays out." He leaned around Patrick and looked at Emma. "She needs more looking after than I do. I think it's taking a far bigger toll on her than anyone. She didn't sign on for all this. He should have told her everything back in England and he didn't!" Mac was almost angry with his boss and Patrick could hear it in his voice. "You take her home and stay with her just like he asked you to." But there he was, still sticking up for his boss.

Back on the road to the house, it wasn't so bad. The car was warm and Emma dozed a little. Her head fell onto Patrick's shoulder and he let her rest there, thoughts welling up inside him. Maybe she would be better with him, like his father had said. As they entered the driveway of the Vega estate, the great iron gates opened. Security was very evident and Emma woke to the sound of the guard's voices.

She sat bolt upright, like it triggered something in her brain. "I won't try to run away again, just don't hit me…" and stared ahead of her, not knowing where she was.

Patrick turned to her. "Emma, Emma. You're safe. It's Patrick. Don't fight me," and he gently shook her back to reality and pulled her to him, holding her there. "He should be with you, Emma, not off fighting dragons for fair damsels in distress!"

Mac raised his eyebrows. "He's fighting demons, Patrick, not dragons, and only he can put this all right, and…he has to do it his way!"

"But she needs him!" and this time Patrick wasn't quiet about it.

"She does. This is where being his son comes in handy. You need to be there for her also, as his son and nothing else. Don Andrea entrusted her to you; always remember that."

How could Patrick forget it?

The car stopped and Patrick helped his step-mother into the house.

"I need to go the bedroom first before I see the children." Emma was pale and drawn.

"I'll help you there. Would you like me to stay for a few minutes, Emma?"

"Yes, please," and Emma looked like she had no idea where she was. She stopped in the hallway, not knowing which way to go.

"This way, Emma," and Patrick ushered her down the hallway to his father's rooms.

Patrick opened the door for her, and she stepped inside. She looked around the room and then straight at the bed she shared with Philip, and she started to sob.

"Hey, Emma. It's okay to cry…let it out…no one would blame you for crying."

"It's not okay, Patrick," she sobbed. "I let Philip down. I remember what happened with Marc! I didn't fight as hard as I should have, Patrick. Marc tried to…" and she went to say it and failed.

"Did he succeed, Emma? Did he?" Patrick had to know for more reasons than one.

And Emma looked at him, her eyes piercing his. She ran to the bed, throwing herself on the luxurious covers and crying until she could cry no more.

Patrick followed her and sat beside her and stroked her hair. He wanted to hold her, wanted to comfort; but she wasn't his. She was the wife of a Don and maybe he should remember exactly who his father was and what power he had.

Chapter 43

Don Andrea was hard to keep up with on a Harley, even with a Ferrari. And his new addiction to pain pills didn't slow him down either. He took the same route as Pauli had and, as it was getting darker, it was harder to see. The sun was going down fast and the lodge was never really that well lit. A little further down the pretty much deserted back road and it came into view. Behind it was the ocean; just a little inlet, but enough to bring a small boat in there if needed.

Philip slowed the Harley and flagged the car down. It was too quiet; not even any birds... nothing. He pulled his cell out and tried the number again. Still nothing. This was not good. He parked the bike and pulled his gun from the back of his jeans, motioning Charlie and Alex to do the same and follow him.

As they got closer, they could see the large oak front door was wide open. Only one window was lit; the others in total darkness.

Philip raised his gun to eye level and the other two men followed suit. He stepped inside the hallway, now halfway expecting there to be trouble. He was right.

In the dim light of the lamp on the dining room table he could see Pauli. He was covered in blood, shot several times as if trying to defend someone. That someone could only be Donna or the baby.

Philip dropped to his knees beside his old and trusted friend.

"No... dear God...No, not you!"

Charlie stood firm and Alex skirted the surrounding rooms, with gun in hand, in search of the shooter.

"Clear."

Philip raised his soldier to his chest and held him there, cradling him in his arms. Sparing him from dying alone. He whispered into Pauli's ear. He tried to tell him that he loved him as his friend. Tried to comfort the dying man.

Pauli flopped back in Philip's arms and whispered so that only he heard.

"Rossi! Philip, I never told her, she doesn't know from me. Rossi suspected you were her..." and Pauli dropped completely back onto the floor with Philip's arms under him, his own hands and sweater now covered in blood.

Vega looked up at the ceiling, and yelled. "Why? Why is this happening? What in God's name did I do to bring this wrath down on the house of Vega? Was stealing someone's wife such a bad thing because I love her? Was it?" Philip screamed at any God that would hear him.

Neither Alex nor Charlie had seen him like this before. His own addiction catching up with him, the last few days, and the loss of his friend were too great a price to pay.

"Andrea, where's Donna and the baby... Andrea, think about them," and Charlie hoisted his friend up from the floor, letting Pauli's body lay there on the blood-sodden wood.

"Leave me alone... both of you!" Philip screamed at them, his voice full of hate. He was out of control, the pills in him and grief taking over. There was no self-control left in him.

Charlie raised his arm and hit Don Andrea Vega hard across his face.

Vega had his gun in Charlie's face so fast it scared him.

"Go on, Andrea. Do it! Just shoot. Do it! Shoot me, if it makes you feel better!"

Philip stared at Charlie and slowly came to his senses.

"Charlie... dear God what has happened to me?" Vega's eyes wide and fearing for his own sanity.

"Too much has happened to you, Andrea; that's the problem," and at that point they all heard screaming coming from outside the lodge.

Donna was screaming and pleading for her life. She had heard Andrea yell and now she screamed for him or anyone to save her.

And then they heard gunfire. One shot and the screaming stopped instantly.

All three of them left the lodge and ran through the clump of trees that protected the house from the ocean. They spread out and ran on out onto the sandy beach, waves gently lapping on the sand and at their heels.

"Donna," yelled Philip. "Donna, where are you?" and a bullet zinged passed his head, narrowly missing him. He ducked down on the sand.

"Andrea, you okay?" yelled Charlie frantically.

"Yeah, fine. I can't see her or Rossi. It's too dark. Anything your way..."

"Boss," yelled Alex, "I have him cornered. He's wounded. Come to your right, past the small pile of rocks."

Charlie and Andrea rushed towards Alex's side. There they found Rossi standing defiant, bullet in his shoulder, arm dripping blood. A look on his face that said 'fuck you.'

Philip got there before Charlie. "You bloody bastard! You killed Pauli. What did you do, sneak up on them? And where's Donna and the baby? Where, you fucking son-of-a-bitch?" and he waved the gun in Rossi's face.

"You think that scares me, *Don* Andrea? You should never have been Don. Damien should. My loyalty was always to him. At least he didn't produce children all over the place!" His voice was older and raspy and full of hate.

"What, like me, you mean? So you know? Damien tell you? That it? Where is Donna? Where? I'll shoot you in cold blood just like I did Marc! Where, Rossi?" Philip was screaming at him.

They heard a faint voice. Donna. They turned to look.

It was then that Rossi made a break for it across the sand and rising surf. Philip raised his gun, took aim, and shot him in the back. Rossi dropped to the sand with Vega firing again and again till his gun emptied its chambers. Charlie and Alex, too. Rossi squirmed in the sand just for a second and then was gone to a better place.

"Time to die, Rossi, you traitorous bastard!" yelled Vega and they left him where he lay, water lapping over his now dead body... left him for the crows.

Philip turned and fled back to where they heard Donna's voice. She lay there, bullet in her stomach, waiting to die. He was the first to her, dropping the spent gun in the sand.

"Oh, my God, Baby! We'll get you to a hospital. You'll be okay," and he tried to hold her, make her comfortable in his arms, pulling her to him out on the surf. He moved stray strands of her hair from her tear-stained face. Pulled her wet clothes round her to spare her pride.

"Rossi shot Pauli. He tried so hard to defend me, Philip. And then I ran with little Andrea. He's over there in the trees. Look after him, Philip, for me, only you…I know you will… I know you loved me…I love you, Philip…" and she closed her eyes and turned her face into his blood-stained sweater, and he clutched her to him. She was gone, never knowing the truth.

Charlie and Alex just stood there, not knowing what to say; neither of them quite comprehending what was going on. Who was who?

Philip picked her up in his arms and carried her back toward the house, tears streaming down his face. Charlie collected baby Andrea from the hiding place and together the three men headed back inside the old lodge. They laid Donna on the couch and covered her with a blanket, Pauli beside her. They had to leave them there and send men back for them… and Emma's car.

No one spoke. No one had to. Words were not needed then. Only questions that were not answered. Now only Philip knew the truth. There had been no time to tell her he loved her also. No time to justify his actions. Now he had to decide to keep the secret and live a lie, or just live.

Chapter 44

Vega didn't even look at the speedometer on the way home. Charlie rode the Harley and Vega drove the Ferrari with VI tags and
Alex holding the baby on his lap. Vega's speed was crazy, over a hun-
dred most of the way. How they weren't stopped was beyond Alex.
All Vega wanted was to get home. All anyone knew for a fact was that
this was Donna's baby. No one, but no one, now knew who the father
was. Maybe that's the way it should stay. But Philip had a feeling that
Mac would not let it rest. If there was a way to find out, he would.
And how would Emma take having a baby of Donna's in the house
with her? All these things and more were flowing through his brain
as he drove home at this ridiculous speed.

He flew into the driveway and thank God the gates opened just
in time, staying open long enough for Charlie Hill as well. As they
screeched to a stop at the main entrance, Anthony was there to open
the doors. Philip went around to Alex's side and took the baby from
him. He held it gently in his arms, like a man born to have children
around him. Little Andrea was Donna's baby and Philip was bound
by honor to look after this child.

Philip carried the child into the house where the Philipa's nanny
stood waiting, ready to greet her new charge. Alex had called ahead.
He handed the baby over to her and now came the hard part, explaining to Emma.

Vega took a long walk down the hall to his suite. It was now or
never. He never wanted to lose Emma. Slowly he turned the handle to their room, hoping to God that Emma understood. He went

through the lounge towards the palatial bedroom and he could hear her voice talking quietly to someone. There was a faint reply. Patrick answered her. The door was just slightly open; just enough so Philip could hear and see them.

Emma was sitting on the top of the bed next to their pillows. Her legs were pulled up to her chin, her hair a floppy mess, and she still sported the clothes from Florida. A box of tissues sat near her, and still she was just as enticing to Philip as she could be. On the side of the bed sat Patrick, handing her tissues when she needed them. He was listening intently to her and trying to comfort her.

Perhaps Emma really would be better with his son, but Philip knew he could never live without her. To tell her the truth now, though, might just push her all the way into Patrick's waiting arms.

The decision was his. Philip would just say Donna's baby was staying there. He couldn't tell her, not now; maybe not ever. The only problem was Mac. He would want a DNA test for him and little Andrea. Would want know if the baby was Marc's child. If it was, then he had a claim. If it wasn't, there was no problem. End of story. Then he thought about Charlie. Possibly he wouldn't let it rest either. Philip knew that Charlie had promised Janine to find her child. Problem number two. He'd cross that bridge when he came to it. Problem number three was Jillie… his daughter proved by a DNA test. And even he wondered now who the real mother was.

Philip turned to leave them and the door creaked as he did.

Patrick spun around, expecting trouble.

Emma shot off the bed, knocking the tissues to the floor, and ran to him with open arms. She flung herself into him and he caught her with more force than intended. He held her there, burying his face in her hair.

Patrick felt like the intruder, but he did wonder what his father had heard. He stood up straight and walked towards the door.

"Patrick before you leave us, I have bad news." Philip faltered. "Pauli is dead. Rossi shot him, and as you can imagine, Rossi is also dead. One more thing," and this was extremely hard for him to say. They could both see it in his face. "Donna is dead. Rossi killed her. And her baby is here with us."

Emma could feel Philip tense against her as he spoke. This was obviously hard for him. A Don wasn't supposed to show feelings.

"We will bring Donna home with Pauli. Bury them together next week. She has no one else." And that was a lie. She had him. "The baby stays with us. As the others know, she named him Andrea." Philip waited for the explosion.

"After you?" asked his wife, looking up into his face.

"After me. I was with her when she gave birth. There was no one else to name the baby after. She didn't know who the father was, so why would she call him Marc or Vinnie?"

Legitimate explanation, but it was raising Patrick's suspicions even further. There were several of them in the room that evening when the Don offered to stay while Donna gave birth. Philip had volunteered.

"I think that's just fine, Philip. Now we have three Andreas in the house," she commented, and left her arms around his waist.

Emma had this awful feeling he was slipping away from her, and that's why she had been crying. And Philip was frightened of losing her.

Philip could feel her breasts though the shirt pressing tightly into his chest and he wanted her. Patrick could see the look on his father's face.

"Patrick, go talk to Mac. Make sure he has everything he needs. And then talk to Anthony about getting Pauli and Donna taken care of. Charlie is with Alex. Make sure they are both comfortable. Ask Charlie to stay the night, would you? First thing in the morning I need to talk with him. And Patrick, Emma's Mercedes is still at the lodge. Pauli used it to get them there. Jillie can wait one more day. I just can't confront her right now. Please take care of it all. Ask Alex to help you. "

Patrick was dismissed, and he knew why.

Philip waited until Patrick closed the suite door. Then he leaned down and kissed his wife. She responded to him the only way she knew how... urgently.

He slid his arms under her legs and lifted her, carrying her across the room onto the giant Vega bed. She looked into his eyes and realized they were once more brown. Gone were the contacts; back were the eyes she loved, deep brown pools with visions of the soul in them.

This time he had no time to be so gentle and pulled off his sweater and unzipped his jeans. Emma undid her shirt and Philip finished the rest for her. To Emma he seemed to be in haste. She wondered then how much he had heard at the door. Maybe too much. Maybe he had heard her telling Patrick about Marc. That Marc had tried twice to rape her and that one time he almost succeeded, and it was only because of Don Santori's interference that he had not been able to follow through. The bruises on her were from that time. Had Philip heard? Would Patrick tell him that he was seriously thinking of leaving home and he had mentioned that he wanted to take her with him, even just for a break?

She tried not to think of these things as Philip's mouth came down on hers and then he carried on down her body. He needed her so badly right now. He didn't stop there and passed on by her stomach and the baby inside her. He knew the child was still there, instinctively. He wanted this child more than anything else in the world. He wanted a son by Emma--this son, the one inside her now. He knew it was a son. Vega just knew. He didn't want any more girls. All they brought him was heartache.

Emma could feel him inside her, an urgency she had not known before from him. He didn't frighten her and she didn't reject him. She wanted it and him. She didn't want gentle. She wanted sex like this right now with him. Urgent and volatile sex. She would take him any way she could get him. She had to keep him happy. She had to keep him, period. He was the only man that she had ever loved, and now she had to prove it him, as he was proving it to her.

Chapter 45

It was ten a.m. before Philip or Emma awoke. They hadn't slept till maybe three, if then. Both had needs to fulfill with each other.

"So much for early morning," murmured Philip and then looked at his wife, curled up in his arms. She was his reason for living.

"Hey, Sleepy Head, we need to get up and showered. I would like you to meet someone...couple of people actually."

"Didn't you already get up?" and her coy little eyes looked into his face as she wrinkled her nose at him.

And that's why he loved her, because she was . . . *her*. Why he had chased her to England and brought her back against all odds.

"Yeah, I did, and tonight I plan to do it again, Mrs. Vega...so let's go shower and you can tell me what else you would like me to do to you!" and he lifted her up and together they showered.

The scar still looked fierce and red as he dried his body. Maybe he should check it out with the doctor, but not today. Today he had serious business to attend to. And he also didn't want to be blonde anymore. He wanted to go back to dark, dark but still long hair. Black dye in this household was easy to find.

In the bedroom Philip asked Emma if she would wear certain clothes today and she was happy to oblige him. He picked everything out. Black lace underwear, black stockings and a very short tight black dress with sleeves. Very high black heels. The waif-like hair only complemented the picture. More than a hint of makeup and she was ready. Ready but hungry. So while Philip dressed, she devoured a plateful of food brought on a tray. Eggs, toast, and orange juice. The sight of bacon made her nauseous, so she passed on that.

Philip had scotch and a bite of Emma's toast. He was also dressed in black; but this time he wore a jacket over tight black jeans, boots and a black silk shirt. Philip never wore the jacket unless it was business, and Emma had a feeling it was.

Noon saw them in the library. Both of them. Only a couple of times had Emma been to a meeting in the library, and never dressed like this. This was serious time. She sat next to Philip as Patrick and Charlie entered the room. Alex was already there behind the boss's chair. Anthony also. Philip had called a 'family' meeting.

They waited till Mac and several other bodyguards were there.

"Close the door." Philip leaned back in the old leather chair, the one kept just for this type of occasion.

He reached his hand out to Emma, who clasped it readily; her legs crossed and her attention very much on her husband. She could sense his tension.

"I have to tell you all that Pauli is deceased. He died protecting Donna and her baby boy. Donna is also deceased. Rossi killed her. I am not going to explain all the details. Charlie and Alex were there with me. Charlie, I have to thank you for your help the last few days. You will find a black Ferrari waiting at your house for you or at least tomorrow it will be."

"Don Andrea...I was joking..." Charlie was shocked.

"I wasn't, Charlie. It's yours." Philip was adamant. "Mac, you will take a few days off to recover. You would have given your life for me and that will not go unrewarded; nor will your actions, Alex." He stopped.

Emma felt him squeeze her hand.

"Patrick, you did a fine job as the next Don, and in a few more years, you will be just that; but for now, I will be pronounced *alive* again. As you can see I have my wife with me. I, we, intended to be here much earlier today than we did, so we apologize but we had a lot to er, discuss..." Philip said it to make a point to more than one person in the room.

Patrick noticed his father squeezed Emma's hand again. He was giving her signals! She uncrossed and re-crossed her legs for affect, and it was certainly working, especially on him. Long black stockings promised a lot but not to anyone except his father.

"Soldiers have been sent to bring Donna and Pauli home. I will personally make the arrangements for their funerals. The baby is here in the nursery, safe and sound, and here he will stay. My wife doesn't mind and baby Andrea will be well taken care of." Philip glanced around the room at the raised eyebrows, but no one said a word. No one dared.

Philip thought that about covered it except for one important thing.

"Alex, is Jillie presentable to visit with us?"

"Yes, Sir. Has been since ten. Would you like me to fetch her?"

"Yes." Vega was back to his one word sentences and that meant business.

There was silence in the room while Alex fetched Jillie. The door opened and Jillie entered with him.

Jillie stood there, not afraid, just defiant. She looked straight at her father, who still held his wife's hand, rather in shock than anything else.

"Gentleman, if you have not already met her, this is Jillie Jennings, my daughter. Jillie I'd like you to meet my wife, Emma Vega."

Jillie stared at the young woman. They were almost the same age. But Emma was sex on two legs, something her husband had made her. Now she knew why her own mother had been of interest to him and why he attracted younger women. She looked at her father. He was outstandingly handsome. She hardly believed this was the same man she was sent to look after. His shirt was open almost to the waist, dark curls could just be seen, his long hair was back to black, and his eyes deep brown pools. And, more importantly, she hardly believed he was alive. But there he sat in front of her, quite obviously alive and full of life.

Shock was written all over her face. She was dressed in sweats and had her hair tied back, but she was obviously his daughter. It was more noticeable today than ever.

"You! You said you were Donna's boyfriend! You sat with her when she gave birth. I should have recognized you and I didn't. They said you were dead. I wanted you to be dead. You destroyed my mother's life and my brother's. And Vinnie's. I prayed you would die, and I thought I got my wish. I heard them take you out that night to the morgue."

It was then that Vega stopped her with a wave of his hand. "As you can see, I am very much alive. Amazing what good makeup, hair dye and contacts can do," and he stood up from the chair, letting go of Emma's hand. "I know you wanted me dead. You wanted my wife dead, too. Before I killed Vinnie, he told me you informed him of everything here at the house," lied Vega. "What I didn't know was how you knew about your baby brother."

"Vinnie told me! Vinnie hated you. You killed his brother, Tony Carbina, you remember him! Shot him in cold blood at your ex wife's house," she screamed at him.

Alex went to restrain her but Vega waved him back.

"I killed him, too, you want to know how? Charlie can tell you. Or Alex. They were there. Vinnie, your boyfriend. You could say he died of shock! And you, what do we do with you?" Vega glared at her. He was exercising his rights as a Don. "And Jillie, you didn't leave your mother to come here. She died a couple of years ago just before I met Emma. So did your step-brother. They were killed in a car crash. I let people here think they were alive, until recently. The authorities notified me. Your mother had me down as next of kin. I had reasons to stay quiet. Only Pauli knew the truth, and your twin brother died the night you were born. I know. I saw the baby's grave when I shot myself. So you see, I did know. You can't hide anything from me. You never went without anything. I paid dearly for you and the one night stand with your mother. But I didn't regret one penny of it, till I found out what you had done. And the question is the same? What do we do with you?"

Jillie stared at him. He had worked the whole thing out for himself but left one thing out. She was angry and now was her time for revenge.

"You won't kill me! Send me away, maybe, but I know one thing you don't want anyone to know. I know that Vinnie wasn't the father of Donna's baby. I made that up about him coming to get her just to scare her," and she turned to look at Mac. "I know who is, though, and so does Mac, and," turning to her father, "Don Andrea, so do you!"

Chapter 46

"Stop, right there. Do not say another word or you will forfeit your life, young lady. You do know who I am, don't you, and you do know what kind of power I have? I can just make you disappear! No one outside this room would know. And everyone here is loyal to me, even Mac. I pay very well, Jillie. You see I hold your life in the palm of my hand, and I think it's best if you go away, maybe Europe."

"Can you send me any further away? Out of your life? But that's what you do with your children, isn't it? Dismiss them!" She was right in his face.

That one hit home. Philip was trying very hard now to control his temper. Patrick could see it and he stepped in.

"I have never known one of us to be sent away. If you are referring to Marc, he was not my father's son. He is Mac's son and everyone in this room knows that. I think, Ms. Jennings, that it was only you that wasn't part of our family. The twins and Philipa are here and baby Andrea." That was really treading on thin ice and Patrick knew it. "I think my father has gone above and beyond the call of duty." Back on track. "I am very proud of my father as are the twins."

Philip looked a little shocked at such backing from his son.

"Well, I guess we settled that. So, which country would you like to go to? You can pick where you want, but you *will* go, one way or another. You came here under false pretenses even though you were checked out and through you we have lost Pauli and Donna. Rossi was always under a certain amount of suspicion. You just confirmed it for me. And now," and Vega looked at his watch, "it's time for lunch, I think. You will join us for one last time and then you are gone." He paused and looked around at Emma. "I had hoped that when you finally came here you might act like my daughter, but that was not the case. Your mother and I had planned that one day you might join us. How do you think you went through nursing school so fast? And got such a clean background? That was all my doing. Unfortunately, I made it too clean and you got into here... and you met Vinnie, something I could not have foreseen. I wonder, would you have killed me?" and Vega reached back and took his wife's hand.

Emma felt his hand tighten round hers. He needed her strength to hear the answer.

"Yes, I would have killed you. That was the plan, but it backfired. Your girlfriend gave birth instead!" Jillie yelled at him.

"Ms. Jennings, Donna was not my girlfriend, in any way, shape or form. And even if she had been, it gave you and Rossi no right to kill her." And now he lost it! "She died out there on a sandy beach, a bullet in her stomach. You did that, Jillie! You sent Rossi after them. Only Pauli and Rossi knew where I would send them for safety... and Mac. And Mac was with me. I killed Vinnie and I killed Marc, personally! And you know, I don't regret one second of it!" She had got to him without his knowing it.

Emma squeezed his hand and then moved closer to him, sliding both hands onto his arm--not a thing one did in the Don's library.

"I think," intervened Emma, "that you should leave now. Alex will be only too glad to remove you and keep you safe and secure till my husband can find a place for you to go," 'hell, preferably', thought Emma. "You and your friends have been nothing but trouble. Your boyfriend and Marc kidnapped me at gunpoint; almost caused my husband's death and Marc nearly caused me to lose Philip's and my baby. So I, for one, would like you to go, now!" and Emma clung to Philip's arm.

Patrick looked at his step-mother. She was the strength behind the man. She had come through for him when he needed her the most and he was truly proud of her, as was her husband. Now Patrick knew why Emma was dressed to kill!

Philip nodded his head. Alex and Anthony took Jillie and marched her to the door.

She had one parting shot for her father.

"It isn't over yet, Don Andrea. It isn't over! You'll see," and she struggled to free herself from their grasp.

"Get her out of here," stated Vega, extremely calm. "Now, let's have lunch in the fresh air. The patio would be nice. Have the children join us," and Philip took Emma's hand again and led her outside.

Vega was way too calm, and they all knew it.

If they had known they would have realized how angry he really was. Here he was trying to put a lid on the whole situation, and there was his own daughter about to blow it off.

Vega sat down at the pool-side table, Emma by his side. Mac and Charlie sat near him and once in a while they would talk among the three of them. Philipa and the twins joined them and Emma left Philip for a few minutes to play with them. Patrick noticed that his father never took his eyes off her. Something was still bothering him.

Vega drank scotch; didn't eat. Everyone else ate. The kids played. Tempting food graced the table. Salads, fresh crusty bread, spaghetti and lots of wine. Ice cream for the kids.

Then Philip's cell rang. He got up, looked to see who the caller was and moved away from the others.

Patrick watched. Whoever was calling him was not making him too happy.

"What does it take? Just do it. I gave you what you needed," and he hung up the call.

Emma slipped up beside him and he encircled her with his arms, and she looked into his face. Something else was going on, something Patrick wasn't privy to. But Emma knew.

Patrick watched them together. They were a perfect couple. How he hoped that both he and Charlie were wrong and that baby Andrea wasn't his father's child. Surely to God Vega could see what he had in Emma.

As if reading Patrick's mind, Charlie approached him.

"He wouldn't have done it, Patrick. Look at them together. He just wouldn't. Renegade he might be, but an honest one, as honest as a Don can be. He's so in love with her, and she with him. I have a theory that I am going to confirm in the next few days."

"Can you tell me?" asked Patrick quite curious.

"I guess. I am going to find Janine's daughter for her." His graveled voice chimed.

"You liked her didn't you? Have to admit my father has great taste in women," commented Patrick still looking at Emma.

"Yeah, he does… of any age. You don't think that he would… well, you don't think he would dispose of Jillie do you?"

"You mean like permanently? No, I don't. She just won't be able to get back here. Maybe a convent or something like that. Probably what he was talking about just on his cell." Patrick hoped he was right. He picked at the food on the table. There was always such abundance, like it was going out of style. But he did wonder, like Charlie, if Vega would just do away with the girl. Not his style, killing women; but on reflection, Jillie was now the only one left who knew the truth.

Chapter 47

The bodies of Donna and Pauli were transported back to the house in Emma's car and sadness overwhelmed the family that evening. Philip went to see them both before the undertaker came and took them away to the funeral home. The funeral was to be a week from the day.

At last Philip and Emma were totally alone in their suite, only a guard outside in the hallway.

Philip waited till they had made love and she rested in his arms. Moonlight glowed through the window onto the bed, casting silver shadows on the white silk sheets.

"Emma, you said today that Marc almost caused you to lose the child. Have you remembered something about the ordeal? Did Marc rape you?"

She moved in his arms and looked into is face, touched his scar and let her hand drift down to his chest. "Would it make a difference if I said yes?"

He didn't even flinch. "No, it would make no difference. He is dead and you are my wife."

"He didn't succeed. He tried twice, but he failed. He couldn't, well you know, and I laughed at him. That's why there are so many bruises on me. I laughed in his face, like you had taught me, to save myself." Tears trickled down her cheeks and onto Philip's still ripped body. She played with the hair on his chest.

"I love you, Emma. Whatever happens, I love you and always will." Philip held her as close as possible to him.

"Nothing is going to happen now. What else can go wrong?" she asked innocently.

"Nothing, Baby, nothing."

Emma froze. Now she wasn't so sure.

They dozed, made love again and dozed some more. Emma woke to find Philip gone from their bed. A note lay on his pillow, accompanied by a red rose. She leaned back in their bed. He'd gone to the funeral home with Alex to make more plans, letting her know he would be back by lunchtime. The rose was to show her his love.

She showered and dressed and made her way to the baby's room. There she found the tiny bundle cared for by Philipa's nanny. Donna's child lay in his cradle, sleeping. Emma sat down next to him, gently rocking the expensive-looking cradle and singing softly to him. He was so tiny and what hair he had was so black. Real Italian looking. The baby opened his eyes and small brown pools of love looked at her. Donna had brown eyes and black hair, but Marc hadn't. He had fairer skin and was blonder like his father and Philip's ex-wife. The baby really took after Donna.

Emma reached into the cradle and lifted the baby out. She rocked him gently in her arms, not noticing that someone had entered the room.

He stood and watched her then and prayed to God that little Andrea was not his father's child. Emma would be devastated beyond belief. Patrick slipped out again unnoticed and went back to his own room. There he made a call.

"Charlie, Patrick Vega. Did you start what we talked about yesterday? You have to do it right? Yeah, I thought you would say that. I just found Emma in the nursery cradling the new baby. I left her there. It will break her heart. Jillie? Yes, she's gone. To an abbey in Switzerland. No, he really did send her there. I told you, he doesn't kill women." Patrick thought about that a moment. And thought of Emma. "Not intentionally anyway. Your car's there? That was fast. Nice? Course it is. How could a Ferrari not be nice? Even I don't have one... yet. Maybe I should ask my father for one. So, when are you going to start looking? Today? Okay. Will you tell me first or Janine? Thanks, that would be helpful, to get a heads up. When did you get Jillie's DNA? Clever! You got whose? Wow. So you have all you need now. I hope it goes the way we want. Let's hope Jillie is her daughter. You think Janine would fetch her back? Me neither. Keep me posted, Charlie. If I can help, let me know." He hung up, still thinking about Emma and the baby. He knew Charlie had all the right contacts to get this done fast… as in real fast, like today.

Patrick walked back to the baby's room and this time made his presence known.

"Good morning, Mrs. Vega," and Patrick's smile was the same as his father's. "Getting in some practice with a baby boy?"

Emma laughed, her smile wide. "He's so cute. Look at his little tiny fingers and that black hair. I hope mine and Philip's son comes out looking like this one."

Patrick almost choked. She might be looking at Philip's son. "Yeah, let's hope."

"Would you like to hold him?" She turned those pretty eyes on him.

"I'm not good with babies. I'll let you and my father do that. He's good at holding babies." *'And calling them Baby!'* Patrick was thinking.

He stayed with her, though, and Philipa joined them, wanting to sit on her half-brother's knee. Playing until lunchtime, Emma left the baby then and went with Patrick and Philipa down to eat. Still no Philip. She began to wonder where he was.

Philip's plans had been delayed, so he was delayed. He was checking his DNA yet again against his daughter's, just to make sure, and he also checked baby Andrea's to him.

When you had the money Philip Vega had, anything you wanted could be speeded up. The results came back just as expected. Some-how he wanted it to be a mistake. It wasn't.

Alex drove them both home. He tried to make conversation with Vega. It didn't happen. Most of the way was in silence. The funeral had been brought forward a couple of days. Philip wanted it over and done and back to a real life. He had said his goodbyes to Pauli and Donna today at the funeral home, and now it was done. Home. Alex and Philip were going home.

Out of the blue. "What kind of car would you like?"

"Sir?" Alex almost used the brake instead of the gas pedal.

"What kind of car, Alex? What good is money if you can't spend it? Especially on folks that have helped you. And careful what you ask for!"

"Any kind is fine, Sir." Alex was shocked. He didn't want a car from Vega. He was just happy working for him.

"Fine. I'll get you any kind of car. And one for Mac, too. Patrick gets a Ferrari, too. He just doesn't know it yet. PV1. Think he will like that?"

"Good grief, how could he not like it?" he paused. "What about Emma's car? You think she should have it back?"

"Already gone. I don't want her driving while she's pregnant. After that maybe," and Philip's phone rang.

Philip opened it. "Hi, Baby. On my way home now. Did you find things to do this morning? Played with Philipa? Lovely, Emmy. And you held baby Andrea? How was that, Em? Yeah, he does have brown eyes, doesn't he? Takes after his ...mother." Philip almost said the wrong name. He glanced at Alex who was drawing a long breath. Philip had to tell her. He couldn't hide it like he wanted to. She would find out sooner or later and later would be worse.

They pulled into the Vega estate. Somehow it looked even bigger today than ever. Vega felt almost too rich. And what good was it doing him? His phone rang again.

"Charlie... you like the car? Good. You want to meet? I think that's a good idea. You have news for me? I have news for you, too. But first I have to tell Emma and I am not sure how she is going to take it..." and Vega hung up. "Sometimes, Alex, money doesn't buy you the happiness you want, except for the woman you want!" And Philip climbed out of the stopped car and went into his house.

Chapter 48

Before Philip had chance to get to Emma he bumped into Mac in the hallway.

"Need to talk with you, Mac."

"Yes, Boss. Something you need?"

"Yeah. What kind of car would you like?" Philip never altered his tone.

"Excuse me?" Mac was shocked.

"I am giving you, Charlie and Alex each a car... or if you wish you can just have the money." So matter of fact.

Mac thought maybe Vega had been at the drugs again.

"I don't need a car, Mr. Vega. There are, like, five cars in the garage if I need one."

"Okay. So what would you like? You did a good job, Mac... and, no, its not blood money! I am not trying to buy your loyalty because of Marc. If anything I would rather it was me than you that killed him. I don't have a conscience." *That came out wrong!*

"Was wondering about that, boss. Do you ever think about it?"

"What?"

"It... when you kill them and I don't. I have topped people for you and it still bothers me. How come it doesn't bother you?"

"Like I said. No conscience." Philip started to walk away and then turned back toward Mac. "Any word from Janine?"

"Wouldn't be me she would contact, Boss. It would be Charlie. They quite liked each other, I gather. Charlie liked her especially. He thinks you have great taste in women. But we all know that," and Mac laughed, first time for days, easing the tension.

"Take it easy, Mac. Take the rest of the week off. Oh, by the way, the funeral is four days away instead of a week. The family is here and anyone that needs to be. I'll see you later." Vega left him standing in the hallway, wondering what the whole conversation had been about.

Philip really needed to see Charlie before Emma, but that wasn't going to happen. He arrived at his suite. Philip dipped his head a little, grabbed a pain pill from his pocket and swallowed it. A double scotch would have been better. Vega entered his suite.

Emma was curled up on the bed, napping. He ran his hands through his hair. Philip didn't want to do this. Why had he slept around so much when he was younger? He sure didn't want to now. All he wanted was the woman on his bed, but he hadn't known her then. Point was she wasn't born then!

Philip sat down on the side of the bed. Emma stirred and immediately looked up at him. All she wore was cut off shorts and T shirt, totally distracting him.

"Hi," she whispered.

"Hi, yourself. How are you feeling? I keep forgetting you are pregnant, Baby. We should get you cheeked out now that you have settled back in the house. I was going to suggest it when we got you home, but it all seemed a lot for you. We'll make an appointment for tomorrow afternoon. What would you like to do this evening? Go to dinner..."

Emma put her fingers on his lips. "I'd like just to be here with you. Just you and I. Have dinner on the balcony..."

She was making this a tougher job by the moment.

"Emma. I have to tell you something. Something I should have told you way back. It's before your time and you always say, '*If it's before, it's none of your business*' and this was twenty-odd years before you." He stood up and away from her. He couldn't tell her sitting there. "Emma, Jillie is definitely my daughter. I had the DNA checked again today, and her mother did die like I said. I also had that confirmed again today."

"I know that, Philip. And you sent Jillie away. I understand why and I am glad she is gone. But it's not that, is it? It's something to do with the baby." Emma sat upright, her eyes wide. She had been dreading this like she almost knew what he was going to say.

"Not exactly. Janine conceived a child round about the same time I left her...I don't know where the child is. I have someone working on finding that out. I never knew, Emma. I swear. It was Charlie that Janine told, not me. He likes her and she him, and baby Andrea is Donna's child and most likely Marc's baby. We are checking that theory out." And he had said it, the truth as he knew it to be.

"Oh, that's all; I thought it was to be far worse." She breathed a huge sigh of relief and jumped off the bed and into his arms. "I thought...well never mind what I thought... doesn't matter now. Yes, let's go out to dinner, just you and me in some cozy little place where I can seduce you under the table. I'll go shower and find something nice and sexy to wear." By "nice" she meant "seductive."

"You go and I'll come join you, Baby. I just have a call to make and I'll be there."

Philip waited until she was gone. He took his cell into the hallway. Speed dialed Charlie.

"Charlie, Philip. I told Emma that Janine and I had a child. I was right wasn't I? I knew I was. How old is that child now? Twenty-seven. Wow. Did you find out who adopted the baby or what the child's name is?" And Philip froze. "Can't be. You are lying," and his voice rose. "Are you sure? I know she's my daughter. I have known for years. When? Way before she came here. And I knew Marc wasn't my son over ten years ago; maybe longer. I didn't know though who my daughter's mother was. Could never trace her back. How come you could and I couldn't? Maybe that was it. I never knew Janine had a baby. Does Janine know? Okay. Let me think. This is all too much to take in."

Philip thumped the wall with his fist. "What a fucking mess. So, that makes sense. I almost told her too, and I couldn't. The girl loved me so much, Charlie. I just couldn't tell her. Now I wish I had. The funeral is next week for them both. Does Janine want to come up? And no, I don't want to talk to her before that. I have an awful feeling that Emma will leave me once she knows all the sordid details. How could she ever trust me? I just finished telling her about Janine having a child. I didn't in all honesty know who it was till this second. Did Santori know? Son-of-a-bitch, the whole time? Charlie, I don't know what to do. I have never been unfaithful to Emma. Not even thought about it. And I never will be. God help me but I really don't know what to do next! You can drive up here? Great. They'll let you in at the gate. And, Charlie, thanks." And Philip Andrea Vega closed his phone and walked back towards his bedroom, a man who was not in control of is own destiny.

And *that* he couldn't handle.

Chapter 49

Philip changed his mind and headed for Mac's room instead. He happened to glance through the hallway window and saw that it had started to rain. Not a good omen. He knocked forcefully on the door. Mac was surprised to see him again this soon but let him in and closed the bedroom door, or thought he did.

"Mr. Vega, what's wrong? You look like you have seen a ghost."

"Maybe I have, Mac. You might want to sit down for this news. You have any scotch in here?" And Philip looked around.

"Sure, Mr. Vega. Double?" Mac went to his own secret liquor cabinet.

"Yeah."

Mac handed him the drink and he downed it in one gulp. Mac refilled it.

"You remember you all thought it was so funny when Donna made a pass at me in the kitchen and then she told pretty much everyone, as I found out, that she was in love with me…and you all had such a joke at my expense? Don't deny it. I'm not blind. Well, I had to back off that night, drunk as I was. She was Marc's girlfriend. Your son's. Oh, I knew for years he was your son. It must have been very hard for you to watch him grow up here. I don't think I could have done it. I knew I had a daughter, too. Jillie. That one was a mistake, but how do you call a child that you made with someone a mistake? You of all people should know that!"

Vega was baring his soul, but to whom better than this man?

"What I didn't know was that Janine was pregnant when I left Florida… with my child. Santori knew I was the father and him we will deal with in time. He had the child adopted. Janine never even saw the baby."

Mac had a horrible idea that he already knew the ending to this story.

"Somehow, and only God knows how, the girl was adopted and she ended up in our house. Her name was…Donna!" Vega walked to the scotch and poured himself another drink. Perhaps being drunk might be a great idea right now. So drunk that this would just be a nightmare.

"So, Mac, that makes baby Andrea your grandchild and he is also mine!"

And that's what Emma heard as she had come searching for her husband, stopping when saw Mac's door open. Just the very last sentence was clear to her. Baby Andrea was her husband's child! Not her husband's grandchild. Philip had never betrayed her. Emma turned and fled back to the room, tears blinding her eyes, her brain in turmoil.

She literally ripped off her dress and threw the high heels across the floor. She ran to the dresser, grabbed some clothes from it and tossed them into the nearest carry-on bag. She donned old jeans and a sweater, grabbed her purse, credit cards and ID. All she wanted was to be far away from Philip. He had lied to her and he had betrayed her with Donna.

When he was late getting home yesterday, she had had Patrick take her to see their own private doctor. She had a present for Philip and that present would now sit on his pillow as a constant reminder of what he just lost. The picture she left Vega was a sonogram of his twins! She had planned to tell him that night when she seduced him..

Emma grabbed her old jacket from the closet, the one she had kept just to remind her of her past life, and now the past life was catching up fast. She slipped into it and grabbed the bag she had packed. Leaving by a side door, she slipped out into the rain, rain that hid her tears as they flowed uncontrollably down her face. She was going to get her car but remembered that Philip had taken that, too. He had taken everything from her, including her pride, and left her with nothing except heartache.

Someone was watching from the kitchen window as she left. Patrick, feeling hungry, had gone to make himself a sandwich. He looked up and looked again. It was Emma he thought he could see. He yelled, but she couldn't hear. He dropped the food onto the marble counter and ran through the house, yelling for his father.

"Patrick, why are you yelling like that? Has something happened?" Alex stepped out into the hallway.

"Where is my father?" His face anxious.

"I'm here, Son," as Philip shot out of Mac's room. "What's wrong?"

"You tell me! I think Emma just left the house carrying a bag. She looks like when you brought her here from England..."

"Oh, my God," and he ran back to the bedroom yelling her name. He dashed in the door of their suite with his son and Mac in tow. On the bed he found the picture, a picture of his unborn children. He clutched it to him, holding it to his chest.

"What did she hear, Dad? What does she know that we don't?"

Philip couldn't even speak.

"Don Andrea was telling me that Donna is his daughter and that baby Andrea is my grandchild and his.... Oh, my God, Boss, that's what she heard. You said he was yours..." There was horror written all over Mac's face.

"Dad, go after her. If you don't, I will. Grandchild is one thing; child is another. Dad, are you listening to me? Go after your wife. Do you want her to walk away? I'll take her from you, Sir. I'll take her, on that you have my word!" Patrick screamed at him.

There was no answer as Vega looked out into the now wet courtyard. He knew he was going to lose her. She would never believe him now. He should have come clean right from the start and he hadn't.

"Dad!" and Patrick left the room, ran through the house and out into the pouring rain of Los Angeles.

In jeans and T shirt, Patrick Vega pursued his dream.

Emma was on foot and it was a very long drive. Patrick was screaming at her in the rain; his voice could just be heard.

"Emma, stop! For God's sake, Emma, stop!" Finally he reached her.

She spun round to look at him with rain and tears mixing in one fine blend of misery. "He couldn't even tell me the truth, and now he sent you. The great Don couldn't even come after me himself!"

"Emma, Emma, calm down. He hasn't done anything wrong! And he didn't send me. I came to get you! I warned him long ago I would take you from him."

"Nothing wrong? I just heard what he said. The child is his! All this time, Patrick, all this time I have stood by him, watched him end people for whatever his pleasure. Do you know what that's doing to me? Do you? I came into his world, and he made me what I am today. I'm leaving him, Patrick. Going home!" She tried to keep walking, but Patrick grabbed her by the arms, stopping her. He wiped the rain from his face, his clothes soaked against his body.

"That's not what he said, Emma!" and Patrick knew he could never hold this woman. She was his father's and always would be. But she needed him now and his stupid pride stood in the way.

Chapter 50

Patrick tried to keep her there. He couldn't. Nothing was going to stop her from leaving. Just then they heard the garage doors go up and the screeching tires of Vega's Ferrari. He shot up the driveway like a bullet from one of his guns and swerved the car to a stop right in front of them.

He opened his door and walked around to the other side of the car.

"Get in, Emma! Get in the car, now!" Vega was more than hostile.

"No, Philip. Get away from me. Don't ever touch me again. I hate you!" she lied, and uncontrollable fear set in and she tried to run away from him.

"I said get in the car! Where on earth do you think you are going? You'll never leave me! I have given you so much, made you what you are today. I mean too much to you." He taunted her.

"I am leaving you, Philip, me and your unborn twins! Boys, Philip!"

Her words hit him hard. He reached in the back of his jeans for his .357.

"Then take this, Emma, and just finish what I started. No one would blame you. Mac figured out what you heard. Donna was my daughter with Janine; little Andrea is my grandchild and Mac's also. Why do you think I brought the child to the house? But you will never believe me; so here, take my gun and shoot me with it... just finish it." His voice calmed and steady, and he realized he really didn't want to go on. He had screwed up so much and now the only woman he really had loved was gone from him. He would never get her back. It seemed it was too late. It was payback time.

Emma grabbed the gun from his hands and held it out in front of her. Her tiny hands shook, but still she held it. She had become like he had made her. A Don's wife.

"I want to leave, Philip. Please just let me go. Please," she begged him, her face trying to hide that she still loved him so much.

"I can't, Emma. The only way you can go is to shoot me! That's your only way out from this marriage and me!" He stared at her, his heart on his sleeve.

"Dad, she'll do it! She doesn't know what she is doing right now," and Patrick could see the look on Emma's face.

Philip smiled. "She knows, Son. I taught her only too well! She is what I made her to be."

Just then the gates of hell opened and Charlie Hill appeared like the angel of death, riding on his black Harley. He stopped dead, the Harley sliding on the wet earth beneath it. "What the fuck is going on?"

And Emma pulled the trigger! Philip stood firm. He didn't even try to move or even close his eyes. The bullet went nowhere near him. She altered her target to hit a tree beyond him. That's how much faith he had in her that she would not try to kill him. He still knew how much she loved him. And he was prepared to die for her and that love.

Charlie jumped from the Harley, leaving it standing in the driveway and rushing to the scene.

Emma couldn't take her eyes from Philip's stare. He had dared her and she had taken the dare. Stripped each other bare. Played by the rules. Made her as hard as he was.

It was then that she fainted and Philip caught her in his arms, the gun falling to the wet ground. He placed her inside the Ferrari, both of them soaked to the skin. Water dripping on his precious car.

"I need to get her home and out of those wet things. Charlie, wait with Mac, so we can conclude this once and for all. Patrick, you and I need to talk at some point. If she still wants to leave, I won't stop her…" and Philip's voice trailed off.

"She'll never leave you now, Sir…not now." Patrick had lost any hope of Emma ever being his. He turned and walked back down the driveway a long road ahead of him.

The Ferrari passed him heading back to house. Philip left the doors open as he lifted Emma out of the car and carried her into their rooms and closed the door. They were not seen again that day, but Mac and Patrick and Charlie talked with Alex. All had stories to tell.

Mac was almost proud he had a grandchild. Charlie was happy that he would see Janine again. Only Patrick had lost everything. Maybe it was time to leave and only return when he was the Don. Give them space; let them become a family again.

But there was one last thing to all be there for. One thing that would draw them together. A funeral.

....

And so on the fourth day of the next month of their lives, limos drew up and took them to the cemetery. Full traditional family honors were bestowed on Pauli; and Donna too was placed in the ground. She was not without mourners. Janine and Charlie stood there, together. Mac also stood with thoughts of the night with Sally and of his son, Marc. Only Patrick stood alone. Alex controlled security, which was more than heavy today as the Don appeared from the biggest limo like the Angel of Death that he was.

The doors opened and Don Andrea walked with a total air of arrogance to the gravesites on the grassy bank. Vega was dressed again head to toe in black, dressed by Armani, long hair and mustache and stubble, obvious power surrounding him. As he stood there, completely in control, he removed his dark shades and his deep brown eyes scanned the mourners, taking note. He looked to his left and there she stood, her waiflike hair pulled tightly on her head and her hand firmly in his. The same tight black dress, black stockings and high heeled shoes as the day he asked her to be in the meeting. She also wore dark shades and pale red lipstick that complemented the picture. She removed her shades and her stunning green eyes gleamed as she looked at Philip in admiration. At last she was home and everyone knew it. Emma was his equal now, she had played his game. She had played by his rules and won.

THE END